Mauricio Velez

Jorge Franco was born in Medellín, Colombia. His books include *Rosario Tijeras, Maldito Amor,* and *Mala Noche*.

PARADISE TRAVEL

PARADISE TRAVEL

JORGE FRANCO

TRANSLATED FROM THE SPANISH BY KATHERINE SILVER

PICADOR

FARRAR, STRAUS AND GIROUX

NEW YORK

www.picadorusa.com

Picador® is a U.S. registered trademark and is used by Farrar, Straus and Giroux under license from Pan Books Limited.

For information on Picador Reading Group Guides, as well as ordering, please contact Picador.
Phone: 646-307-5629
Fax: 212-253-9627
E-mail: readinggroupguides@picadorusa.com

Designed by Jonathan D. Lippincott

Library of Congress Cataloging-in-Publication Data
Franco Ramos, Jorge.
[Paraíso travel. English]
Paradise travel / Jorge Franco ; translated from the Spanish by Katherine Silver.
p. cm.
ISBN-13: 978-0-312-42596-8
ISBN-10: 0-312-42596-1
I. Silver, Katherine. II. Title.

PQ8180.16.R28P3713 2005
863′.64—dc22

2004062823

Originally published in 2002 by Grupo Editorial Random House Mondadori, S.L., Barcelona, as *Paraíso travel*

First published in the United States by Farrar, Straus and Giroux

First Picador Edition: January 2007

10 9 8 7 6 5 4 3 2 1

To Jaime Echeverri, my teacher

To Enrique Santos Calderón, my saint

PARADISE TRAVEL

I could easily have died that day at dawn after I got lost, not only because death itself stood in my way, but because I craved death with a passion. I remembered and finally understood all the times Reina had said: Let's just kill ourselves, but after saying it so many times, nobody paid much attention anymore.

"Let's just kill ourselves," she'd say angrily whenever things didn't go her way.

I wasn't worried about only Reina's life but about everybody's, especially mine that I took such good care of, not for any very good reason, maybe just that pessimistic love I always felt for life, a love that lasted until that night when I was the most desperate human being, when for the first time I thought: Better dead than alive and without Reina. But it was my memory of her strange ideas that made me believe I could take one more step, and then another.

I knew when I started running that I was starting to lose her, and that in the twinkling of an eye I could also lose myself. While I was running away from the policemen, I pictured her, her angry mouth shouting: Marlon, don't go out!

But you also have to figure in my anger, and when I went out that night I never imagined I was going to get lost in the world's biggest, most intricate labyrinth, doomed to having as my last memory that angry expression on Reina's face, her yelling at me like my mother used to when I was little: Marlon Cruz, don't you go out!

I yelled back at her and left. We yelled at each other all the exhaustion and silence we had been keeping bottled up inside us ever since we'd decided on this madness of coming to New York to find our future.

"New York?" I asked her.

"Yes, New York."

"Why so far away?"

"Because that's where it is," Reina said.

It was her idea. As a rule, all the ideas were hers. I had a few of my own, but only Reina's got anywhere, and this one was already well on its way. By the time she told me about it, everything had been decided. She didn't even ask if I agreed.

"We're both going," she said.

She went on about all the opportunities, the dollars, the chance to earn a good living, live a better life, get away from this shithole.

"In this place we haven't done anything, we aren't doing anything, and we aren't ever going to do anything."

To finally have a place for the two of us, where we could get ahead in life and even have children, she continued. While she was saying all this, her eyes shone and she looked so sincere I actually believed her; there was so much determination in those eyes, they even scared me.

"But it's so far away and we've never been there before," I told her.

Reina squeezed my hands and pressed her mouth up against mine. Instead of eyes, I saw two glassy blotches of different colors darting back and forth, as if they were searching for the fear behind my eyes. She started talking in a different tone of voice and even the rhythm of her breathing changed.

"We're both going," she repeated. "Or do you want to stay here, like your mother, like your father, like my father, screwed like all of them?"

She said this quietly, her lips glued against my face, her body pressed against mine as she breathed warm air out through her nose; she wasn't angry, just determined, and she pushed her breasts into my chest with each breath she took so I could feel exactly what I'd be missing if I stayed.

"We're both going."

But she didn't kiss me like I thought she would; instead she pulled her face away from mine and dug her fingers into my hair. She left them there and stared at me, as if she was waiting for me to tell her something different from the *yes* she was already counting on, maybe even some new idea that would strengthen her plan, something that would make her different-colored eyes keep shining.

"But I don't speak English, Reina" was all I said, and she pulled her hand out of my hair.

It was all her stupid idea, and I told her so when we arrived. All our money was gone, the address where we were supposed to go didn't exist, and things just hadn't turned out how we'd expected. We had been suffering in silence the whole trip. We were so scared we barely slept at night, and we couldn't rest during the day, either; I kept wondering if we'd ever get where Reina wanted to go. So I threw it in her face.

"It was your idea," I said to her angrily.

"Yeah, I know," she said. "Because you never have any of your own."

I complained that this dump had nothing to do with the place she made me dream about, the one she described to me when we imagined the life we'd lead when we got here. She was the one who told me about it as if she'd already been, as if she'd gone on ahead of me to get everything ready for our arrival: It's a freshly painted apartment with a view of the river and the Statue of Liberty, on the top floor with a small terrace and a little garden, two chairs where we can sit and watch the sun set over New York City. She told me about the dog we'd have and take for walks after work, who'd look after the apartment while we were out. She told me about the spotless kitchen full of modern appliances, and the white bathroom with a huge white bathtub we could climb into every night and make love in. We're going to make love every night, she told me, and I felt butterflies in my sex and thought: We're both going.

But the real-life room was like a jail cell they rented to us for our last few dollars, and we took it because we didn't have any choice. We didn't find Gloria, her cousin, the one who had sent the pictures, the one who messed with Reina's head, the one who told her: *Ven prima*, come, there's money here and work for everybody; and she sent a picture of her apartment, and it was pretty great, and another of her standing next to a car, but now I wonder if that was even hers, and another with a dog in the snow next to a snowman with two twigs for arms, a carrot for a nose, two black things for eyes, and everybody in the picture smiling, but looking so strange, distant, like apes in the North Pole.

"We're going to see snow, Marlon," Reina said, hugging herself as if she could already feel the cold.

I thought: Yeah, right, you can pass for a gringa because even though your eyes are kind of weird, they're light colored, and your hair, too; all you need is a little dye to be a real blonde. But I'm so much from here—that's what I thought, but didn't tell her—so totally from here that I don't want to go there.

"Look at these pictures Gloria, my cousin, sent me." She showed them to me like they were tarot cards and she was dealing out our future.

She showed them to me every day because she kept them in her wallet, and she'd pull them out on the bus and in the street, so she could enjoy the apartment, the car, the dog, her cousin Gloria's snowman. She showed them to me at the airport, whenever I was afraid, all along the way from there to here, even though we had been forbidden to bring photographs. She carried them around as if they were her documents, the visa they didn't give us, the money we spent, the passports they made us throw away.

"But your cousin Gloria," I said to her in that dump, "gave us the wrong address."

"Maybe we memorized it wrong," Reina said in her cousin's defense.

"And the phone number, we memorized that wrong, too?"

That's how we spent the last of our money. They answered in English and Reina said: Gloria, Gloria, pliz, but she got such a barrage of words from the other end that it scared her.

"Take it, see if you can understand," she ordered me.

The whole thing almost made me laugh. She said: Maybe we got the wrong number, let's try again; and I warned her: Reina, this is the last of our money. But Reina gave me a dirty look, dialed, and again the same thing: Gloria, pliz, and the same tape in English. Reina finally gave up: I think it must be an answering machine.

"Let's go up to the room," she said to me, "and we'll call again tomorrow."

I asked her: With what? And she told me, One of our neighbors will let us use their phone; but I didn't think there'd be more than one in a run-down place like that. And when we got back to the room, I felt like I was drowning.

"It was your idea."

"What did you think?" she said. "That we were going to stay at the Hilton?"

"No, at your cousin's."

Maybe it was because of the size of the room, but when we talked to each other it sounded like we were shouting. Reina said to me: I'll call Gloria tomorrow; we'd better get some sleep; we haven't slept in days. I asked her: What are we going to do, Reina? But she didn't answer, so I asked her again in a louder voice: What are we going to do?! Then she gave me a look that told me to go straight to hell, and since I had one cigarette left, I decided I would go outside to smoke it, get some fresh air, think, take a walk so I could think. I slammed the door behind me and she opened it.

"Marlon, don't go out!" she shouted.

As I went running down the dark stairway skipping two steps at a time, I could still hear Reina yelling: We don't know where we are, Marlon; we don't have any papers. I reached the hallway, gave the telephone that had stolen our quarters a dirty look, then went out. I'd forgotten my jacket and I got a blast of cold wind in the chest, but when I lit the cigarette, I felt a little warmer. I looked up, trying to find Reina at one of the windows, but I wasn't even sure that our window looked out on the street, or even that we had a window. I looked across the street and saw a brightly lit billboard where I saw the one word I understood in English: Queen. I knew this word because that's what Reina means in English.

I started walking and the fresh air made me feel better, even though it was so cold. I started to think that Reina might be right: after a good night's sleep, we'd see things more clearly in the morning. Maybe the next day we'd find Gloria and everything would work out. I had already gone halfway around the block, the cigarette was burned about halfway down, and my upset was about half gone. I decided to walk all the way around the block, then go tell her how stupid I had been. I tossed the butt on the ground and was turning around to go back to Reina when I saw that the butt had landed right at the feet of a policeman and my heart froze.

I looked up at him and he spoke and I didn't understand a word he said. He pointed to the patrol car that I hadn't seen, or maybe he was signaling to his partner, who was talking on the radio. I think I mumbled something and I think he said something else I didn't understand but that was enough to make my feet decide on their own. He turned to talk to his partner and I dashed off in a panic, a panic that was pushing me faster and faster; I was knocking down people in my way, but I kept running. I turned and looked behind me and now the policemen were running after me, not very far away, clearing a path through the crowd. My feet were flying and the cars screeched to a stop as I ran across streets. Their lights made it look like I was running through a merry-go-round. The policemen were still chasing me, but my fear had given me wings.

"Marlon, don't go out!"

While I was running, I was remembering the order I should have obeyed. I kept running, the two policemen on my tail, the cars between my legs, and the lights blinding me, but I kept running. *Marlon, don't go out!* I turned more corners and I kept running, not knowing how much longer I could go on; but the honking horns were chasing me, I saw the policemen getting closer and closer, and I thought of Reina and of God. Suddenly, just as I was crossing another street, I heard a dull thud; I've been hit, I thought, but it wasn't me, it was one of them, one of the policemen flew through the air near me, almost next to me, so the other one stopped, looked at his partner on the ground, and then looked up at me; but I kept running, and I ran on past gigantic walls and neon signs and buildings that disappeared into the sky, through a sea of human beings who didn't seem to pay much attention to a man running away with nobody running after him.

I kept running many more blocks until I got to a dark corner, wherever it was that my despair led me and my feet followed. I didn't know how far I had run. There were lots of streets and a long bridge, and the whole time I was filled with panic but not as much as at that moment when I looked around with watery eyes and didn't recognize anything; all around me there were warehouses and signs, but I couldn't understand them. I was still gasping for breath, and I remembered something I always said to Reina: I've never been there; I don't speak English.

And then there was her shout: *Marlon, don't go out!* With time it began to fade into all the other shouts of New York City, but I tried so hard not to lose its echo because it was the only thing that kept me going, that kept me looking for Reina.

"My name is John Roberts and I'm going to be driving this bus for the next eight hours," the bus driver says in English over the loudspeakers. "You've got the rules right in front of you, but just as a reminder . . ."

John Roberts begins to recite the rules, but nobody is paying attention; they're all used to this country where everything is prohibited but people find a way to do it anyway.

"I don't want to hear any music. I don't like music," John Roberts says. And he doesn't want to hear loud talking, he doesn't want a mess, and even though it should be obvious, he's going to say it anyway: "I don't want no booze or cigarettes on this bus."

He stops giving out warnings long enough to pop a piece of candy into his mouth.

"I've got friends in the police who'd be very happy to assist me in throwing anybody who breaks the rules off this bus," he says as he chews his candy.

One passenger sticks out a finger as if he'd like to stick it up John Roberts's ass. I look at the woman sitting next to me to see her reaction, but she is busy putting away her bags. She is a large black woman, well on in years and with a generous amount of flesh on her bones; she is trying to fit herself into the not-very-generous seat.

"Last but not least," the driver says, "our next stop is Baltimore. If we don't hit any traffic, we'll be there in three and a half hours."

"Well, I'm hungry already," says the woman traveling next to me. Then she asks me, "Aren't you?"

What with this business of seeing Reina again, I've forgotten to eat. I didn't even eat when I got to the station. I didn't budge from the gate where they told me to wait. It isn't going to happen again; I'm not going to get lost again now that I know where she is. I'll eat when I get there; maybe she'll want to eat something, too—that is, after she recovers from the shock, and if the excitement of seeing each other again doesn't ruin both our appetites, like it's doing to me right now. I'll have a meal with Reina one year and three months later. One year, three months, and five days later.

I say to the woman sitting next to me:

"No, I'm not hungry yet," and then I add, "I'm going to wait until I get to Miami."

She lets out a laugh that makes other people on the bus turn to look at her. John Roberts also looks through his rearview mirror. Her teeth amaze me: they'd be big for any mouth, and they're spotlessly clean and white. She keeps laughing as she shakes her head from side to side, probably as she adds up all thirty hours of the trip.

"My, my," she groans through her laughter. She places her hand on her chest and tries to stop herself from laughing.

Her nostrils grow larger as she tries to catch her breath. She says: Oh, my son. Then she doesn't say anything else. She closes her eyes and begins to hum. I lean my head back and look outside, and I see myself reflected in the glass, watching as New York City gets farther and farther away. It seems to move off slowly as if it knew I was going to meet her, or maybe so that I'll remember what I'm leaving behind, what I managed to do on my own and without Reina, the woman I left Colombia and came to this country for.

Reina, the girl from the *barrio*, that's how they talked about her, or as the one who left and then came back a long time afterward. She left with her mother and returned without her. She came back with her father, both of them wearing long faces.

"What happened? Did the *señora* die?"

Nobody died. The *señora*, the mother, left. Mama raised her eyebrows and screwed up her mouth; she didn't say anything, but we all knew what she would have liked to say. This time, that is, she didn't say anything, not in front of us anyway. My friends kept insisting: Reina, the one with the two different-colored eyes, but I couldn't make a connection between the one who had just arrived and anybody I had known from before.

"I don't know who you're talking about," I said.

"Reina! The one who has one eye of one color and the other eye of another color!"

"I give up. I don't know who she is."

How was I supposed to recognize her if she was a little girl when she left and a grown woman when she returned, if she was all ugly when she left and a knockout when she came back? She didn't look at all the same. If it weren't that I remembered her father, I would have thought they were pulling my leg.

"The same one who . . . ?! But she doesn't look like her at all."

Yes, she returned fully grown and developed; at least that's what we saw when we watched her get on and off the bus, walk to the corner store, walk to church on Sunday.

"And here I am, still sleeping alone with my radio," said Juancho Tirado, drooling.

So that's who she was. The one who played with all the other neighborhood girls when she was little; they played hopscotch, jump rope, hide-and-seek. We used to steal their candy and pocket money, and we never let them play with us or join our gang. No girls allowed, only women, Eduardo Montoya asserted. We are girls, the girls all said at once.

"So pull down your panties," we said, and they ran off screaming. Then they'd return a few days later to look for us again.

"Now we're women."

"So come and take a piss with us." And again they ran away terrified, screeching as if we were a bunch of lunatics.

Reina was one of the ones who screamed and ran away. She wore a short jumper, had dirty knees, messy hair, and crooked teeth, and she was annoying and mean like all little girls are, obnoxious like all kids, stinky, loud—you know, a little girl. Nothing like the Reina who showed up ten years later.

"Queen Reina reigns," Carlitos said, pushing down on the bulge in his pants.

"Why did she come back?" I asked as we watched her carrying bags out of the store, as I made up an answer to my own question because Juancho Tirado, Carlitos, and Eduardo Montoya had taken off like lightning bolts to offer to carry her bags; and she let them help her, a little flustered at first, but finally with more smiles. I stayed there, leaning against the wall, watching those three dogs pacing around her, thinking that I was losing a lot of points by staying where I was, that one of them would get her in the end, just thinking, as I watched them walk away, all in a huddle, laughing and flirting, until I went stiff like a board, because just before they turned the corner, when I could see only their backs and I already knew everything was lost, Reina turned around and looked at me, not like she was looking at any old thing; no, more like she was looking at something she wanted to look at.

"You want one?" my traveling companion asks me and places a paper bag, open, under my nose.

"No, thank you," I answer without even asking what it is.

"They're muffins," she explains. "Blueberry muffins."

I glance in the bag, but the smell is stronger than the sight, the smell wins out because it makes me close my eyes. Then memory wins out over the smell as the scents of my own house suddenly swirl around me, the scent of the patio and Mama's kitchen, then some instinct wins out over memory, and like so many other times, I get this unbearable urge to go home.

"I made them myself." The woman's husky voice brings me back. Before I make a decision, she insists, "Come on, you haven't eaten anything since we left. Just try one."

I reach my hand in and the texture is like the smell. I bring it to my mouth and she waits for my reaction. I nod and chew as she says, "I'm Charlotte."

I think I've gotten lost in the flavor. I wonder if what I heard was her name, where she's from, or where she's headed; then to make matters even worse, she starts spouting more women's names.

"I'm Charlotte, I'm from Virginia, and I'm going to Augusta, in Georgia."

After a year my English isn't that bad, even though I learned it in the school of hard knocks, for survival. That's why I always think of English as the language of necessity.

"And you?" she asks.

I give myself some time before I answer and while I finish chewing, so I can figure out what her name is and put off dealing with something that should be so simple but is so difficult to face, something that seems so dangerous and daring, like saying: My name is Marlon Cruz and I am from Medellín, Colombia. Because then I'm always afraid of the look on the other person's face, that they'll act like I just said I had a deadly and contagious disease.

"How interesting," Charlotte says, and I'm thinking she wants to hide her astonishment, her horror, because I have this feeling there shouldn't be anything interesting about being from Medellín, Colombia. But then she adds:

"I've got a niece there, in Bolivia," and I smile, realizing, not for the first time, that most gringos don't even know where Medellín is, and, as far as most are concerned, I may as well be from Asunción, Maracaibo, or Panama. For them it's all the same. I do feel some kind of relief when I see that where I'm from doesn't scare Charlotte off, because she offers me another muffin and asks:

"Do you have blueberries in . . . ?"

Again, I feel like saying to her: It's okay, just say it, the name won't explode, then I remember she probably just forgot such a strange-sounding word and I politely remind her: Medellín. And I wonder: Blueberries in Medellín? And I laugh because I wouldn't even know how to say "blueberries" in Spanish, and so that she doesn't think there's something weird about my laughing, I explain to her:

"Yes, yes, we do. Anything is possible in Medellín."

I think: Anything besides forgetting. Even I, who got so lost, even I haven't been able to forget—no matter how hard I've tried—who I am and where I come from, not because I'm ashamed or want to deny anything, but so that I can start from scratch, with no regrets and with my feet solidly planted on this side of the earth.

But as it was, I forgot precisely what I shouldn't have forgotten: my steps as I escaped; my frantic, terrified, demented steps through a totally unknown city.

I thought I'd find Reina that same night, that it was a simple matter of retracing my steps and looking for the trail I'd left behind during my escape, shift into reverse, go back in time, or, if it had been at all possible, just get over my fear and collect my thoughts. I told myself: It's not so hard to get back; it's just a question of calming down and remembering. I kept repeating to myself: It's not that complicated; it's not impossible. I started walking very slowly, looking around and trying to recognize something, anything, and I remembered a warning I had heard:

"Everything looks the same there."

It was Carlitos who said that, who always seemed pissed off

whenever we'd talk about the subject. He was never in favor of us going. He repeated endlessly: You're going to eat all the shit you've never eaten before.

"But it'll be gringo shit," Reina told me afterward.

"Maybe Carlitos is right."

"So, stay here with Carlitos," Reina suggested.

I squeezed my memory trying to find my way back where I had started running. I forced myself to remember something, anything, a doorway, a sign, maybe the bloodstain left by the policeman at the very moment—or just before—he died.

At least a scent, I insisted.

A color, a sound, some clue to a specific place, so many things a city has that you can remember; so many things and I couldn't find even one. I suspected, also, that I was walking in circles, like you do when you're lost in the jungle.

Then I stayed put in one place to see if she would come and find me, just like that first time when I found her eyes on me, without asking for them, that first afternoon when my friends ran after her, and it was Reina who ignored them and turned her attention to the guy leaning against the wall and wondering why Reina had come back to our neighborhood.

"It seems her mother left them," they told me later.

"That's why they came back?" I asked.

"Maybe they want to forget."

"Nobody comes back to forget," I answered.

Not even me, who months later wanted to find the exact spot where I had gotten lost, the very heart of the labyrinth. To come back the way you might come back to a grave to tell the person in it: You are dead and I am alive; to tell him: Let me live, I don't have any choice. To come back to kill the dead, so it would be impossible to ever run into him, to stamp out any hope for a miracle. I looked a lot for that place, after a while not so I could find my way back to Reina, but so I could forget it. But those streets had been permanently erased from my mind, streets where I vomited in terror, wandered around frozen and dazed, crept up to the oil drums and bonfires of the other street people.

I don't know how many days I stayed in this trance, because when you get lost, other things, like time and space, get lost, too. The few moments I do remember are as lost as I was, as blurred as the people who looked at me with disgust, some who gave me food and even spare change I never asked for. I started seeing Reina hiding around corners; I saw lights and sirens and policemen; I saw skinny cats scurrying between garbage cans, scavenging for the same things I was; I heard other languages and Reina shouting: *Marlon, don't go out!* I heard Mama's voice and saw Papa's face, looking at me sadly; I heard noises and saw confused shadows and Death holding a scythe and saying to me the same words Reina used to say: Let's just kill ourselves. Then I'd hear a different voice, maybe my own, encouraging me: Keep walking, you'll find her soon. Sometimes I believed it, and other times I realized that I was delirious, that's why I still don't know what was real and what wasn't real, that's why I doubted what I was seeing when I saw the sign and read what I had no logical reason to read but that made me think I wasn't really there, that I had never really left, that my people and my house and my friends and even Reina had to be very close by. That's why I thought, I'm crazy, when, after a few days of searching, I saw the red lettering on the yellow background on the big sign that read TIERRA COLOMBIANA.

You were a horrible sight, the most repulsive monster in the entire city of New York," Pastor Gómez stated, wrapped in the poncho he took off only after summer was well under way. "You stunk like a devil in the morning, like a gorilla's yawn, like a faggot's underpants, like a piece of rotten shit, like a cat's fart."

That's how Pastor Gómez described the deplorable state I was in when I entered his restaurant, and he wasn't just saying it to make excuses for the force he used to throw me out.

"You don't have to exaggerate, Don Pastor."

"What I don't have is the time and the words to tell it like it really was, and so far I've mentioned only the smell. Then there's the way you looked when you burst in here, and how you acted."

Pastor Gómez said that a madman walked into his restaurant, a raving lunatic, to quote him, and his wife thought it was the devil himself because she saw me foaming at the mouth and jumping around in a way no human ever has before or ever will again.

"Exaggerations, Don Pastor," I said. Then I asked, "Where would I have gotten the strength?"

"You had the strength of despair, son," Pastor Gómez said. "Three guys grabbed you to throw you out and you fought them off."

Don Pastor described how his customers ran off in terror, some locking themselves in the bathroom; how Patricia fell to her knees, crossed herself, and began to pray.

"In all my years here, I'd never seen anything like it, son," Pastor Gómez said. "I don't even remember seeing anything like it there in Colombia."

The one who didn't remember anything was me. It felt like Don Pastor and his wife were talking about some other person. Whenever they'd talk about it, I'd even laugh because it was like they were talking about somebody else, and I still believe that and I can even prove it: that guy wasn't me.

They also told me that the employees picked up brooms and pulled out their fake machetes to get me out, but that I stood up to the broom handles, the kicks, even the punches in the face, and that I got tame only when one of them shouted: Call the police!

"Those were the magic words that made you quiet down, and then you began to speak in a civilized tongue," Don Pastor told me.

One of the guys said: He speaks Spanish; and another insisted: Call the police; and the one on his knees this time was me, pleading, my palms pressed together and in very clear Spanish: *Por favor, no, por favor, no.* They almost didn't realize I was crying, because the second the tears left my eyes, they got sucked up by the filth on my face.

Even so, even though I'm sure that guy wasn't me, Marlon Cruz, the one now riding on this bus on his way to see Reina, even though I wasn't that guy no matter how much they swear to me I was, even if it was somebody else, I feel sorry for him because he honestly believed he would find himself when he entered that restaurant that he thought was his country, his home. I can almost feel what he felt when he saw that sign and smelled that unmistakable smell of frying empanadas and heard those familiar voices with that same tone and the same accent, and for a minute he thought they were all there, his father, his mother, maybe even Reina or Carlitos or Juancho Tirado. That's why I can feel how desperate he got when they tried to throw him out, as if they were asking someone who was just waking up from a nightmare to go right back into it after experiencing that unbelievable relief of being awake; that's why it's like a knife in my soul every time I think about that other guy who could have been me. Even if Pastor Gómez and his wife say it was, I won't accept it: that wasn't me who was in that body.

The same thing happened to me the first time I was lying on top of Reina on her couch, biting her lip. I couldn't believe it was me she was giving those long kisses to while Gonzalo, her father, was taking a nap upstairs in his room with the television on full blast. We were taking advantage of him losing his hearing, and I was taking advantage when I stuck my hand under her blouse to see what I could grab hold of.

"Slow down," she said.

"I'll go as slow as you like," I offered.

"You'd best be getting home."

"But we're just getting started."

"That's exactly the point."

That night I had to satisfy myself the way Juancho Tirado showed us years before in the school bathrooms when we thought he was just taking a piss like we were, but no way; he showed us how to do it to ourselves. The next day I said to Reina:

"Sorry if I went too far yesterday, I'm not really like that. I thought about you all night."

"What else did you do?"

I turned red, especially when she started laughing real hard and said:

"You're going to grow hairs on the palms of your hands."

"Who taught you about all that?"

Everyone, of course, has his or her own Juancho Tirado. And especially Reina, who found out about grown-up things when she was a little girl. That's what they said about her and that's what Mama said:

"Seeing as how she didn't have a mother . . ."

She did have a mother, it's just that she left. With another man, they said. Mama also said:

"With other men."

But that didn't necessarily mean that Reina was like that. She even went to a good school. She even used to go to a Catholic school and had nuns as teachers. But Mama insisted:

"Clothes don't make the nun."

I didn't pay any attention to Mama. Reina was Reina, end of story. There was no reason for her to have to carry around her mother's history her whole life. Even though she did think about her when we went through San Antonio right after we crossed the border. It was night and she was half asleep; me, on the other hand, I didn't even dare put my head down, even though it did feel like lead. We were riding in the car—Caleña, that's what we called the woman from Cali; Ping, the Chinaman; Reina and I—and Caleña and Ping were fast asleep, and so was Reina, but in fits and starts; things had been going wrong for days now. It was like she was having some kind of premonition that things were going to get even worse, because in her sleep, Reina let out a sharp cry: Mama! I said to her: Calm down, Reina, we're almost there. Where? she asked me anxiously and only half awake, but what could I tell her since nobody knew, not her or me or Caleña or Ping or the gringo, not God, not nobody.

"How could we have known, Don Pastor, if neither one of us was ourself?" I asked him.

"What? Say that again?" he asked, taking his hands out from under his poncho.

"Say what again?"

"You going on with that same old story, son, about how you weren't you, about how whenever you're up to your neck in some problem, you aren't you, and now you tell me that girl, Reina, also wasn't that girl?"

"That's how things are, Don Pastor."

"Just that easy?"

"Not so easy, Don Pastor."

Much less easy for those of us who were looking for an easier life outside our own country. Just the opposite: it's been a whole lot more difficult. Maybe less thankless, but definitely more difficult.

"You can see for yourself, Don Pastor, that the guy who landed in your restaurant wasn't the same one I am now, can't you?"

"Well, yes, but . . . no."

"You see, Don Pastor, that it's possible for something to be and not to be?"

"To be or not to be," he stated solemnly.

"That is the question, Don Pastor."

How could that have been me, my same self, who kissed Pastor Gómez's feet, begging him not to call the police, who fell on my knees and threw my arms around his; because even he wasn't his same self when he angrily asked his employees to get me out of there, and they all attacked me at once, trying to throw me out with kicks and punches, until I said: That's not necessary, I'll go out on my own. That is, anyway, what Pastor Gómez told me I said to them in a voice that wasn't my own, either; and that like a dog—or worse, more like scum, because here dogs live better than any poor Colombian—I dragged myself out the door, and there, on the sidewalk, I curled up, crying and making sounds like some kind of wild beast.

"Get him away from here, he'll scare away my customers," Don Pastor ordered.

They threatened me again, and again they warned me: Go away or we'll call the police; and as if I'd been struck by a lightning bolt, I jumped up, crossed the street, and fell onto the facing sidewalk, where I could see Pastor Gómez and his wife's restaurant and where I could smell the empanadas.

"I do remember the smell, Don Pastor."

The guys from the restaurant told me that I didn't move from there for the rest of the day, curled up on the sidewalk across the street, not budging, staring hard at the door of the restaurant. The guys also told me that Don Pastor kept fretting, looking out the window constantly to see if I was still there. That's where I stayed until dark. Then, according to what the guys tell me, Patricia, Don Pastor's wife, went into the kitchen before closing up and grabbed some cold leftover empanadas. They say she wrapped them up in a napkin and, while her husband was locking the door and lowering the grate, she crossed the street, walked over to me, and next to my feet left the package that saved me from starvation.

They say she went back and said to them: That poor boy is going to freeze. And they all looked at me but nobody said anything, except Don Pastor, who placed his hat on his head, wrapped himself in his poncho, and said:

"He would have been better off if he'd stayed in his own country."

Maybe we lost each other that very instant Reina turned around to look at me, leaving my friends high and dry and feeling betrayed by this woman they already considered theirs, the bigheaded fools.

"That's the thanks we get," Eduardo Montoya said to me later. "We carried her packages, invited her out, we made her feel like a queen . . ."

"They're all like that," Carlitos chimed in.

"You treat them like princesses, then they go off with the first asshole they meet," said Juancho Tirado; then he added, making an exception, "I'm not talking about you, Marlon."

"He means some other asshole," Eduardo added.

I laughed, too, but if I could have foreseen what nobody can see—that moment when we start to get lost, or that instant when we set out on our own, for better or for worse—for sure I wouldn't have laughed like I did, like a winner laughs, when my friends were coming down on me for Reina being interested in me. But laughing or not, I would have done what I did and had to continue doing ever since that moment I was sure that Reina had turned to look at me the same way she kept looking at me until that night she angrily begged me not to go out.

When things were first getting started with Reina, it seemed like I could never get rid of my friends. The four of us were always hanging around her house or her school. At first I didn't mind; being in a group gave me confidence, or at least an excuse for hanging out there, on the street, waiting, but always pretending that I wasn't when she showed up.

"Here she comes," the first one who saw her would say.

"Don't all look at the same time!" I'd warn them, but nobody listened, except me, who might as well have been talking to myself, looking in the opposite direction from where Reina was coming, while those three studs started panting, falling all over themselves, smiling and flirting, and there she was, totally aware of all the fuss they were making, pushing out her chest and even changing the rhythm of her steps, obviously enjoying all the attention.

"Where's Queen Reina going?"

"Good-bye, boys," Reina answered.

I'd stay off to the side, afraid to show my face, pretending that my mind was somewhere else, but really my chest was as cold as ice.

"We'll go with you, Reina."

Until finally I got up the courage and pretended I had dropped in from nowhere, and once I was standing there in front of her, I pretended I was smiling because I was surprised, but it was really from excitement, joy, just plain gratitude for so much beauty.

"No thanks, boys, I'm not going far," Reina said without stopping, her different-colored eyes piercing me, flirting with me for as long as she could without twisting her neck out of shape or going past the limits of what she thought was decent.

"Your wish is our command," any one of the three would say, and I'd lift my hand and try to look natural as I waved good-bye. We watched her walk away, like she was evaporating into the street, and we couldn't help wondering if her appearance so close to us had been an illusion, like the wind itself.

Afterward they all made fists and punched at me with more real anger than I was used to from my friends.

"What a brave sissy you are!" all three said. But I didn't care: why should I? I just laughed.

"You're laughing to yourself," Charlotte suddenly says to me.

"What did you say?" I ask her, taken by surprise.

"You were laughing to yourself." And then she adds, "And that's good. These days if somebody laughs to himself, they say he's nuts, but nobody knows that he's laughing with God, and He's laughing, too, believe me, He laughs when you laugh with Him."

I try to imagine how God's laughter would sound, and I can't tell if it would be an occasion for joy or trembling.

"Did I tell you I was going to see Him?" Charlotte asks.

She says it so naturally, like she was going to see her uncle, even more straightforward and simple than me telling her: I'm going to meet Reina. Her tone sounds so familiar, you'd think God was just any old Tom, Dick, or Harry.

"And you're going to . . . Miami?" she asks again.

To Reina, I think, to my goal, the conclusion of my search, where the movie says "The End," and where this fatigue and exhaustion are finally over.

"To Miami," I agree, and smile.

Charlotte nods and gives me a smile, bigger and whiter than mine because her mouth is as big as two of anybody else's. Then she closes her eyes and I notice that even though they are huge, her eyelids are even bigger. She hums a song, maybe so she can be alone with God. I, on the other hand, feel something similar to what I've felt many times over the years, because I think that maybe Charlotte is really going to meet death, because that also happens a lot: dying and God are sometimes the same fate.

"Are you okay?" I ask her out of the blue.

"What?" she asks, returning from her melody.

"Nothing," I say, excusing myself. "I was talking to myself."

"So that means you were talking to Him," she says, and her smile can't fit on her face. Suddenly her hoarse voice sounds almost like a child's and she says, "The only one here is Him, because He is ubiquitous and beautiful. Go on, keep talking," and she leans her head back and continues to hum, still smiling.

I lean my head back and look outside. It's getting late. I think about the times I did speak to God and how much intensity I placed in each word I said to Him. I think about the answer I waited for, about that waiting that convinced me that there was no silence in the world like God's silence, even though I always remembered Mama saying: God makes a racket, too; and Aunt Marlén agreeing and giving a suggestive wink: Oh boy, and what a racket! All because she found a man when she was already in her fifties and after she'd already made her peace with dying a virgin and an old maid.

I envy Charlotte: the one she's looking for is always there. To find Him she doesn't have to waste her time on predicaments and false scents, tears and panic attacks in the middle of the night; she doesn't have to walk around with her eyes staring out of her head, looking for God in every face, like I've been doing this whole year, looking for Reina in every face within my limited field of vision and even, sometimes, turning around suddenly just on the hunch that I am being followed or, like happened so many times, running toward some woman who, from far away, I could have sworn was her, but once I get up closer, all my excitement drains away and my hopes crash and burn. A few times I would stare at them, rescue little pieces of Reina: sometimes her hair; sometimes her body, the way she moved; maybe a smile or a certain expression around the mouth—so many things that remind us of someone but are nothing other than thin air. So many, so similar, but not one was Reina.

"How many times you figure you've walked by each other in the street?" Pastor Gómez asked me.

"Impossible, Don Pastor," I answered him. "I always look at every face I pass."

"Your eyes can deceive you, son."

"But not my heart, Don Pastor."

No. Reina never walked by me. She was never in the same place as me at the same instant. Maybe one minute before or after, but never at the same time and in the same place.

"Maybe you never saw her, but the other guy did," Pastor Gómez insisted, in a teasing tone.

"What other guy, Don Pastor?" I asked.

"You, when you were the other guy."

The guy who ran out and got lost, the one who roamed the streets, the wretch in the gutter, the one so weighed down with sadness that he walked around staring at the sidewalk in front of him, trying to avoid stepping in the dog shit, not caring about his life or anything else, not even about Reina maybe crossing paths with him, just walking aimlessly through a city that is impossible to really get to know.

"Maybe, Don Pastor," I admitted, thinking that maybe there had been some moment when life had taken advantage of me staring at the sidewalk, of my constant setbacks and disappointments, one of those moments when Reina's suicidal words, *Let's just kill ourselves*, had been echoing in my head. At one of those moments, life might very well have placed her in my path so that I'd walk right by her just when I was stepping around the shit. Life is like that a lot.

"But there was also her, Don Pastor."

"What do you mean, son?"

"Her eyes," I told him. "'Cause even if mine were distracted, maybe hers would have seen me."

"What if she was also walking around in a daze? Not to disillusion you, but . . ."

I remember that Pastor Gómez made a face to finish that sentence, but since I needed something more than faces, I insisted, "But what, Don Pastor?"

"But nothing, son," he said, then added, "just that sometimes life is like that."

Then life doesn't know about all the times I wanted so badly to look up from the dirty streets and meet her eyes looking happy and surprised. Many times I did look up, hoping for this happiest of coincidences, but the only thing I found was, to put it into the words of Don Pastor, life's teasing gaze.

"But it wasn't always like that, son."

"I know why you're saying that, Don Pastor."

He wasn't referring to the one time I saw Reina after we lost each other, because nobody believed me, not even I did when I was face-to-face with her, because then I thought it was just life playing its little tricks again, and I didn't manage to convince myself until a few seconds afterward, when it was already too late, that Reina and I had just run into each other in New York City. Don Pastor was referring to that morning when I was sitting on the sidewalk in front of the restaurant, apparently having decided not to budge from there, and I looked up and saw Patricia Gómez handing me a blanket and—like adding a cherry on top of a sundae—giving me a generous smile. The guys told me the part about the blanket, but the part about the smile I made up afterward.

The guys also told me that she did it against her husband's wishes, that he stood in the doorway and stated firmly:

"That guy is going to imbed himself in us."

But Patricia was only paying attention to when the light would change so she could cross the street, even though Don Pastor still wouldn't admit defeat.

"And then we won't be able to get rid of him even with gasoline!"

But Patricia acted like her husband's shouts were just one of the many noises of the city. They say she came up to me, standing up straight and very sure of herself, and handed me the blanket, but that I just sat there, paralyzed, staring at her, maybe because I was scared or maybe shy, but that it was a while before I took it from her, and that once I had it in my hands, I unfolded it quickly and wrapped it around myself; and that in spite of the grime on my face, the guys said they could tell I was relieved. I must have been, because how else would I have made up Patricia's smile?

Little by little I was losing my fear of being under one of Reina's sieges. I was getting used to the volleys she shot from her weird eyes, used to meeting that stare and matching it when I looked back at her. Everything that was so strange at first I got used to, until I didn't have any reason anymore to keep making as if I wasn't interested; I definitely was, and how! Why should me and my friends keep pretending that nothing was going on when Reina's very eloquent eyes had already made their choice?

Finally, one afternoon, my friends weren't on the street corner to watch her go by. I was alone, my hair greased and perfumed, pacing around in a circle three steps in diameter and with a proposal pacing around inside my head: Can I walk with you, Reina? But when I saw her from far away with the afternoon sun behind me and shining right on her, I forgot my proposal and everything else I'd been thinking about while I was spinning around on my own axis.

"Why are you alone?" she asked without anesthesia.

"Just one of those things," I told her.

"Well, what do you know!" Reina exclaimed. "How weird."

I agreed, as if the situation really was weird; I still had my hands in my pockets.

"What happened to your face?"

"I cut myself shaving."

"Are you just going to stand there?" she asked.

"No . . . well, no," I answered like an idiot.

"So walk with me," Reina said, and started walking ahead of me.

I stayed a few steps behind her, like her squire. Now I remembered the proposal I had prepared, and I swore at myself for not remembering it sooner.

But I didn't always act like such a total idiot, because a little confidence goes a long way and everything Reina did was telling me that her mind was made up, that now she would even allow me to wait for her outside her school.

I also remember that from then on Reina started exercising her wings so they would be strong enough for when she needed them to fly. She already had an idea in her head, and a country, and I remember feeling disappointed because I thought I wouldn't have Reina for myself for very long. She was in her last year of high school and her plans were to study "far away from all this shit."

"In the United States," she told me confidently.

I'd already spent a year and a half trying to get into the university, a public one because in the private ones I didn't have a reserved spot or the money or the pull you needed to get in. But when the public ones weren't on strike, they were bankrupt, or you had to get a recommendation from some politician, or be the most talented or gifted of all the thousands who wanted to get in. I didn't meet any of those criteria, and my only good fortune so far—and it was huge—was that Reina was interested in me.

"You see?" she'd say to me. "Here you can't do anything even if you want to. They're going to leave you there standing in line until they just happen to feel like letting you in."

I had no answer for that. Colombia eventually leaves you without arguments. That's why I kept quiet, and also because I couldn't even consider an option outside the country. I didn't have enough pesos, let alone dollars. I had to admit that Reina was right and I'd keep standing in line until they decided to accept me, keep talking my dad into letting me slide on paying him for room and board, keep working as a clerk in the fabric store to earn a few pesos so I could take Reina out to the movies, or give her a ride in a taxi, even though I did like to watch her walk.

Now I close my eyes so I can hear Reina's steps, that music each of us makes when we walk, as unique and personal as our fingerprints, but more connected to our own histories than those lines on our thumbs. Because it keeps changing as life keeps going, as the bad times and all the problems roll along, with all the difficulties and the sorrows. That's when steps that once sounded easy-does-it end up sounding like slaps on old leather. But even everybody's dragging steps sound different, and maybe Reina's rhythm, just like mine, has gone through some changes; I'm sure we don't walk like we did a year ago, not because we're old, but because we're tired. That's why we'll have to look each other in the eyes, so we can recognize each other, because it won't be enough that we're just there, in the same place. There's a strong possibility my foot will shake when I see her, and she'll have to squeeze my hand and tell me: Keep your foot still.

"Keep your foot still," she ordered me when that woman, Fabiola, showed up with her smile-for-all-seasons that always rubbed me the wrong way and told us:

"Okay, kids, everything's ready; we're sending the paperwork to the office this afternoon. Let's hope everything goes well."

"Why wouldn't it?" Reina asked.

"It's not as easy as you think; they're not giving visas to many people these days. Things are very complicated."

"What do you mean?" I asked.

"The lawyers will let us know what our chances are."

And then, with that everlasting smile etched into her face like it was just another feature, she added, "If it doesn't come through, we'll talk."

"What about?" Reina asked.

"About what to do next," she clarified, almost in a whisper, even though from our faces she could tell we had no idea what she was talking about. "There's always something more we can do. But let's not get ahead of ourselves. I'll call you on Monday and let you know how things are going."

And without us asking for it, she came up to us and stamped a couple of smiling and perfumed kisses on our faces.

"I don't like that woman," I told Reina once we were outside.

Reina was upset. She was walking quickly and the expression on her face was the opposite of Fabiola's.

"She's always smiling," I pointed out.

"Who?" Reina asked.

"Fabiola."

"What's that got to do with anything?"

"I don't like people who are always smiling," I said. "Because you never know what's going to happen when the smile goes away."

"Look, Marlon." She came to an abrupt halt and turned to face me. "Don't you turn into a bad omen, like a black cat or a broken mirror. That woman is doing everything she can, and considering all the money we gave her, she's got to get us our visas."

"That's what I don't like," I interrupted. "Nobody ever charged anybody that much for a visa."

"Exactly—all the more reason why she'll get it."

We kept walking and not talking. The sun was so strong my forehead was sweating, and I saw little beads on Reina's upper lip. I didn't know where we were going and I didn't dare ask. I just followed Reina. After walking for about ten minutes, I felt her fingers brush against mine, and without stopping or looking at me, she took my hand and asked me:

"Got any money?"

"Like for what?"

"Like for a Coca-Cola."

I told her I had enough for a Coca-Cola and a pastry. So we went into a café, sat down next to each other, ordered two pastries, two ice-cold sodas, and while they were serving us, Reina squeezed my hand, looked at me, and asked:

"What are you afraid of?"

I looked at her and didn't say anything. I clenched my teeth so that nothing stupid would dribble out of my mouth, so I wouldn't say: Life is giving me a run for my money.

"I'm not afraid of anything, Reina," I finally managed to say.

"You don't have to come with me, you know," she said.

"No way."

"I could go first, get settled, look around, check things out, then . . ."

"Then what, Reina? Then you won't even remember I exist."

She caressed my leg, my thigh; she let her hand drift over to the swelling in my crotch, but she quickly passed over it, like she was still embarrassed, or like she was surprised to find her hand there, or so it would seem like a mistake. Her caresses didn't help my foot stop shaking.

Today, before getting on the bus, it felt like it wanted to shake, but I managed to control it. But sometimes I'm not so careful and it does shake, especially when some city is getting left behind. Anyway, you don't see the cities, you only see their names, and you can only imagine what they're like as you pass each sign: Baltimore, Richmond, Petersburg. The same thing happened with Reina, who left me with only her name.

"Petersburg," I repeat out of that habit I was forced into, repeating words so I'd learn English. Because at first, just like during the Creation, everything was without form, and void. It was as if nothing existed even though everything was there, because for me nothing had a name. And if it wasn't that fate, oddly enough, took me to Queens itself, where there are thousands of people who speak Spanish, my story would have been very different, because thanks to that coincidence, I was able to say to Patricia Gómez, according to what they tell me I said to her: *Me llamo Marlon Cruz y estoy perdido*.

That's what I said to her after a while, probably once I'd gotten used to her regular visits with something to drink and almost always something to eat, and when her smile and her kindness finally made their way into my darkness, and I felt that motherly affection from her that always makes you feel good, that you always kind of miss and even old people long for.

Yes, they say that's just how Patricia looked at me, and at night even more sadly, when her husband was lowering the grate and everybody was putting on their coats and getting ready to leave and, from the other side of the street, she'd look at me all motherly and sigh, and then she'd bring me her usual offering.

Until that evening when she went back all emotional and excited, choking on my words.

"He said his name is Marlon, Marlon Cruz, and that he's lost!"

Everybody looked through the window as if my name had changed something. Everybody except Pastor Gómez.

"So what difference does that make?" the old man argued. "He's still just as filthy, just as disgusting." Then he called out an order:

"Get to work, everybody. To work!"

But apparently he didn't say anything to his wife; and even though he looked at her angrily, she pretended not to notice, because she kept looking at me over there on the other shore, with her hands over her mouth, and then, still puzzled, she said:

"He talks just like us."

That's when Pastor Gómez finally stopped whatever it was he was doing, turned to her, his eyes firm and decisive, and said:

"Come, let's go to my office."

What Don Pastor called his office was a tiny room with a telephone on a desk that was jammed in so tightly the door couldn't close.

Nobody knew anything for the next few minutes until Patricia reappeared with the same expression on her face as Don Pastor had on his going in. Or as Giovanny Fonseca, one of the guys, said: Patricia came out with a man's face. The rest of the day, the subject wasn't mentioned; in other words, they didn't say any more about me.

"But whatever they didn't say with words, they said with their eyes," Giovanny explained to me with his own eyes bulging out of his head.

Because between one look and another everybody was wondering what had happened in Don Pastor's office, and giving each other one look here and another there, they guessed what had been talked about, and from the look in Patricia's and Don Pastor's eyes, they understood that they hadn't come to an agreement. That's why they figured they wouldn't hear Patricia's normal voice or see her with her hair down for many days. Before you ask, Giovanny said, Don Pastor doesn't like women to wear their hair up; only if they're in the kitchen.

"Well?"

"Well, eyes don't lie, *hermano*, and for three days, besides being a waiter, I had to be a messenger, because the same thing happened that always happens when women get pissed off: they decide not to talk, and they go around giving orders. 'Tell the *señor* this,'" Giovanny continued, imitating Patricia's voice, "'and tell him that, tell him I'm going out, tell him I'm leaving early today.'" And then, in his own voice, "And Don Pastor, right there, hearing everything, but she's pretending like he isn't there, and I'm repeating like he hasn't heard. And it was all your fault."

"Mine?!" I jumped. "But I wasn't even me at the time."

"Yeah, right."

"Yeah, right yourself. Continue the story."

Since Giovanny liked telling stories, he dropped that put-down tone of voice he used when he was blaming me for everything, and with a lot more affection in his voice, he continued:

"On the third day Patricia arrived with a different look on her face, an expression of triumph—all smiles and laughter—her head held high and her hair down."

"Go on."

"Patricia looked like she had just ridden right over Don Pastor with a steamroller, because he showed up with his face all flattened out, and one of the guys, like a jerk, asked him, 'Hey, Don Pastor, what's with the face?' and Don Pastor snapped at him like a mad dog, and said, 'Don't ask stupid questions, it's the only one I've got,' and kept walking toward his office. I'm sure he would have loved to slam the door if it wasn't for that corner of the desk that got in the way."

Giovanny paused to laugh, change his position, and scratch his eyes, but I was egging him on: Go on, go on. I was very interested in my story, as if it belonged to somebody else, which I still say it does. I've said so many times: That crazy guy wasn't me.

"Well, *hermano*," Giovanny continued, "that morning nobody said anything, but we were dying to know, and we kept making signs to each other, showing how anxious we were to find out. But everything came clear slowly, because it was Patricia herself who let us know that on that very day your life was going to change."

"Why?" I asked enthusiastically. "What did she say?"

"Nothing, she didn't say anything, but just after she arrived, she went into the kitchen, asked for pots and chicken and vegetables and I don't know what else. Whatever else, it was clear that she was the one doing the cooking. Then she left the pots cooking on the stove and called over Óscar Iván, and said to him, 'Come here, Óscar Iván, and give me a hand.' Of course she didn't say what for, but they walked toward that little room in the basement where they keep all the junk, and before the stuff in the pots had a chance to boil, that little room was cleared out, all the garbage was out in the street, and soon the whole restaurant was smelling of soup."

At that point in the story, it was me who needed him to slow down. I told Giovanny: Wait a minute. But he was already off and running.

"But we still didn't understand what was going on with the room. I was making hand signals to Óscar Iván, trying to get him to let me in on it, but he shrugged his shoulders like he didn't know anything, either, so the only thing to do was keep working and watch Patricia out of the corner of my eye."

Then he explained about how the *señora* took out some plates, arranged them all carefully on a tray. How you could see the pleasure on her face while she poured the stew into the bowl, and how she made sure the bread was hot and the juice was fresh, and how very carefully she covered everything with a cloth and went straight out into the street, right past everybody's stares and Pastor Gómez's angry glares.

"The truth, *mi hermano*, is that because we were looking at him, we missed the exact moment she crossed the street, went up to you, went down on her knees, and offered you enough food for you to eat to your heart's content."

"And did I eat?"

"Not everything. You left the bowl."

Giovanny also told me about how Patricia talked to me while I ate, but that I only answered with my head, how sometimes I shook it to say no, and sometimes I nodded to say yes, but at no time did they see me open my mouth to do anything other than chew. They were watching everything from the window, taking advantage of the fact that there were no customers and Don Pastor was distracted, glued to the other window, grumbling, sighing, and saying:

"Women are the shits."

Maybe he said that because he knew what his wife was

planning and guessed what we couldn't: that this bowl of soup would be the appetizer to a meal that would bring many more surprises, to a decision that would split my story into the "before" and the "after" my life is divided into.

From that moment on, my story took on a different name, and Giovanny and the other guys, and even Pastor Gómez himself, would remember that moment as the day the Virgin appeared before me.

So then this woman, Fabiola, appeared, with her permanent smile and makeup all the way down her neck. She turned up and told us:

"Sorry, kids, but it looks like they're going to turn us down for the visa."

"You, too?" Reina asked, whether innocently or cynically I'm not sure.

"What I mean is . . . ," Fabiola said with a smile, but ended up saying nothing.

Reina let her head drop and her hair fell over her face. I looked at Fabiola with hatred and anger, with a strong desire to say to her: What are you smiling about? But I held my tongue for Reina's sake.

"So now what?" Reina asked, her face hidden behind her hair.

"All is not lost," the smile said, and then added, intoning each syllable, "There is still hope."

"Let's get out of here," I said to Reina, grabbing her hand and pulling on it.

"No." She stopped me and turned to face Fabiola. She asked, "What can we do?"

Then, for the first time, Fabiola stopped smiling, and after closing the door and making sure we were alone, she took on a mysterious air that she probably learned at the same school where they taught her to smile. Then, with her eyes wide open, her hands tense and twitching, she said in a mysterious whisper as if she was reciting a lesson, "We can't talk here."

Slowly she reached her hand over to a scrap of paper, and without taking her conspiratorial eyes off us, picked up a fountain pen, jotted down a number without looking at what she was writing, and said in a voice we could barely hear:

"Call me tonight at this number."

"Who . . . *what*?" asked Reina.

"Call me," she repeated, a little louder, "at this number . . . tonight," and she slid the piece of paper across the table under her hand. Reina picked it up. We knew when the scene of suspense was over because the smile reappeared on her face, as if somebody had pushed a button to turn it back on.

We left without speaking, without even looking at each other, without knowing if the other one was filled with rage or disappointment. Reina kept her eyes on the ground and walked quickly, about a yard in front of me, the way queens always walk: in front of their escorts. Finally, I couldn't stand it any longer.

"Uh-uh," I refused from the bottom of my throat. She didn't react, or hadn't understood what I was trying to say with those grunts. So I tried again: "Uh-uh"; and this time it worked. Reina stopped, leaned wearily against a post, and looked at me. She was crying.

"Nobody is going to ruin my dream," she said. "So be very careful what you are about to say."

"Reina," I stuttered, "that woman . . . that woman can really mess up our lives."

"I'm in this to the end, Marlon, just you wait and see."

I went up to her so she could cry to her heart's content, so she wouldn't feel so alone in her struggle, but I repeated my concerns:

"That woman, Reina."

"That one or another," she interrupted. "Nobody, you understand, nobody."

We didn't speak again until we got to her house. On the way she stopped crying and I even thought she'd gotten over her upset. Still, she said:

"I'm going to the embassy myself and I'm going to ask for a visa."

"But you heard what she said, Reina," I told her. "There's no chance they'll give us one."

"Stay for dinner," she told me. "I need you to entertain my father while I call Fabiola."

I'll always remember that night because now I'm sure that it was that very night when we started to lose each other, at the moment I said to her: Yes, Reina, you can count on me. I said it without much conviction, but I said it, and she, her heart still pounding and her ear hot from the call she'd just made, she, anxious but smiling, said to me:

"It will all turn out fine; there's a little risk, like in everything, but it's going to work out for us."

"What are you talking about, Reina? I don't understand you," I said to her, but she began to compensate me for my support with wet, passionate kisses on my mouth and neck, heavy breathing, running her hand under my shirt, and touching, now without any shyness, my swelling that had grown under her rough caresses, each of us on top of the other, dressed and in a hurry, trying to keep quiet because Gonzalo was in the room next door with the television on.

I wanted to take off her clothes, but she resisted: Not here, she said to me, panting, not here. Throughout the struggle, I had been rubbing against her leg like a dog, then I came. Then we let go of each other and even before the stain appeared on my pant leg, Reina said to me between spasms:

"In New York we'll go all the way."

In the meantime, it would be halfway sex, but sex, after all, with the woman I loved.

Like I said, we began to lose each other that night, lose track of each other because we were deceiving each other by making false promises. I gave Reina a yes that was really a no but that she understood the way she wanted to or the way it was convenient for her to; and just in case, and to leave no room for doubts, she added, still out of breath from our frustrated sexual interlude: This is just a preview; and I smiled as I stared at her swollen nipples under her blouse. A preview, she said, of what we're going to do every night in New York. And I, who had no other thoughts than of her and who felt so full of myself because I had scored the one everybody wanted, I told her: Yes, Reina, I'll go with you. I agreed radiantly, not knowing that from that night on, while we were still in Medellín, I had already begun to sketch out the paths of the labyrinth.

"Tell me, what does it feel like to be crazy?" Giovanny Fonseca asked, curious.

"I don't remember," I said.

"Try to remember."

I tried, not because he asked me to; I'd been trying for a long time, but I could never salvage anything. The sensation was of falling asleep at some point, maybe in the street, which I do remember. Also the cold, the vomit, the hunger, and that sensation of being lost, but that's when I was still sane; afterward it was like I fell asleep and everything was some kind of endless night, delirious, without any memories and without any answer for Giovanny Fonseca.

"You should have asked me when you first saw me come in," I told him. "That was your chance."

"What're you talking about, *mi hermano*? Don Pastor wouldn't even let us look at you."

"Don Pastor is a funny one," I suggested. "Did you notice how he changed toward me from one minute to the next?"

"No," said Giovanny, "he's always been a decent guy, it's just that he doesn't want to take any chances with his money, his hard-earned dollars. You really did seem dangerous."

"So who talked him into letting me stay at Tierra Colombiana?"

"Patricia," Giovanny explained to me. "She worked on him until he had no other choice."

"They're all the same, those women: forces of nature."

"Patricia must have been a force of nature and a half, because in the state you were in, I wouldn't have let you in, either."

"Thanks a lot."

"Seriously, *hermano*, you were a sight. Who knew what you were thinking about at those moments."

"No idea," I told him, "but the list was probably long. Maybe I was thinking about my parents, maybe Reina's father, maybe even Reina herself, or her cousin Gloria. Who knows what I had in my head at that moment."

Whatever it is crazy people have in their heads: some fixed idea, a fear, a pain that doesn't go away, a memory that won't fade, an obsession, a desire, a broken heart, a dream. What do I know about what crazy people play on their tapes. I didn't even know what I was playing on mine.

So, when you're not who you are at those moments when things aren't going quite right, it's precisely then, if you're lucky, that somebody comes along to help you get back inside your body and get your mind back in gear so that body and mind can stop wandering around looking for each other, like Reina and I have been doing; or like the souls of the dead that come back, that aren't yet resigned to dying, or are scared of the bright light at the end of the tunnel, or because they were lucky enough to feel the sadness of those they left behind; or as Aunt Marlén would say, because it wasn't their turn yet.

That's when somebody shows up, somebody a true believer might call an angel, and they tell you what they tell me Patricia told me: Stand up and follow me. And the guy who wasn't me was scared and asked her: Where? And she, according to what they tell me, repeated: Let's go, Marlon, come with me. And the guy who wasn't me began to return to his body, like someone who's dying and sees himself lying there, and sees people standing over him and crying and holding the dying person's cold hand, and sees them lower his eyelids and place his arms over his chest; and he watches everything as if from far away, as if he had nothing to do with the guy who just died. Right at that moment, if he's lucky, this somebody shows up, maybe an angel, and says to him: Come with me, go back to your body and offer those people a miracle.

"Ven conmigo, Marlon."

But I could barely look her in the eyes, I was so spooked; I just babbled nonsense and shivered from cold and misery. She bent down over me, sitting so pathetically there on the sidewalk, and grabbed my cold, filthy hand, but I pulled it away because I was scared. Apparently I asked her: Police? And apparently she said:

"Nothing is going to happen to you. There won't be any police. You are going to a warm place, where there's no rain or wind, and we're going to feed you."

She said that I looked at her with so much gratitude and that my face lit up. Then she took me by the arm to help me stand up, and she felt like she was lifting a bag of air, a bunch of rags that struggled to keep their balance. They say I lost my balance and fell, but she pulled me up again, wrapped one arm around my waist, and grabbed my shoulder with the other one so that my skeleton wouldn't just crumple.

Step-by-step, like someone carrying his own sick shadow, we made it to the corner to cross the street. Everybody was watching us from the window, all of them speechless, amazed, with their snouts squashed flat up against the glass, not giving a thought to the customers or to the empanadas that were getting burned; everybody, including Don Pastor, who was swearing as he grumbled and made angry faces that fogged up the glass.

Everybody, including the people walking by on the street, was watching when the traffic light turned green and Patricia crossed the street with me. And people sitting in the first row of cars and others that came from the other corner, and the ones alongside us, they all turned their heads to watch a dead man walking. All this in a city where you can see everything, where curiosity doesn't exist, where nobody looks farther away than their own two feet, because maybe very few of them have had the privilege of seeing somebody rising straight out of hell.

"You stank like a horny devil, like shit and sulfur, like a nun's fart, a girl's sweaty—"

"Don't exaggerate, Don Pastor."

"If you don't believe me, ask the boys."

Everyone nodded, as if once again the description of how I stank was something they could all agree on.

"We'll never forget your aroma," Don Pastor emphasized.

But she just kept walking slowly with me toward the restaurant. When we got there, we stopped, and Patricia knocked a few times on a metal door at street level. The door opened quickly and I saw a metal staircase that led into a basement. That had been part of the agreement she made with Don Pastor: The customers don't see him, he doesn't show his face, he doesn't leave his room, he goes in and out through the storeroom, and he gets out of here as quickly as possible.

"Down you go," Patricia told me.

She helped me keep my balance, almost pushing me, but always reassuring me with friendly words: There's nothing to be afraid of, my boy, you'll be better off here, keep going. I walked slowly down the stairs, watching the sidewalk reach my neck, thinking what my friends would have said if they could have seen me: Look at Marlon, how the earth is swallowing him up.

When they closed the door I couldn't see anything, but it smelled like food. It took me a while to get used to the indoor light, but Patricia was my guide, so I let her lead me into a small room. On the floor was a mattress and on one of the walls was a calendar frozen on February 17, 1985.

"Okay," she told me, "here's where you'll stay today."

She told me later that I seemed confused as I looked around the room. We were alone because the employees were forbidden to get near me, and even Pastor Gómez said that he'd only go there to put on the chain and padlock.

"They locked me in?" I asked when they told me that part of the story.

Yes, because that was also part of the agreement. Nobody knows that guy, Patricia. What are you thinking, that we're going to leave him here alone for a whole night? And she answered: This isn't a jail, Pastor. And he answered: But it isn't a hotel, either. They argued back and forth until they finally reached a compromise: He can stay, but under lock and key.

Patricia tried to help me understand it in other terms, but she waited until I had settled down a little. First she talked me into going into the bathroom and taking a shower.

"First you've got to clean yourself up, *mijo*."

She led me to a bathroom that was so tiny it reminded me of one on an airplane. Even so, it had everything: a shower, soap, and shampoo. Patricia said to me: There are clean clothes in this bag, then you can use it to put your dirty clothes in. She pushed me in, gently, and closed the door.

If I had seen myself before that, I never would have gone in, or if I'd known what I would find in the mirror that was as small as everything else in the bathroom, but big enough to see what had so horrified the others, and now, at that moment, gave me a shock. There, right in front of me, was the best proof of what I have always said. There was the guy I once was not, but who I started to be from that afternoon on—even if we were different—because never before or after had I seen anyone so different from me when I'd looked in a mirror. And if it wasn't because we both moved our heads at the same time and touched our faces to recognize ourselves, or because of the panic in both our faces, I would have thought that somebody behind that mirror was playing a trick on me. I would have sworn it if I hadn't seen him and heard him say her name: Reina. We said it at the same time.

When I started to take off my clothes, I realized I had shit in my pants. I was smeared with shit from the waist down. But the real shit would come later, when I started to wake up under the shower. Slowly I started to see the whole movie playing in front of me, scene after terrifying scene that had brought me there, or at least, as much as I could remember. I felt even more terrified than when those things were actually happening; I relived each moment, second by second, like they say happens to somebody who is about to die. Just like that night, I saw myself walking through dark streets, then reaching other streets that were lit up more brightly and where there were cars rushing past. I saw myself looking from side to side, terrified; again I experienced the moment I decided to turn right or turn left, and I got to where there was more light and some buildings; I saw people looking at me, probably wondering: Why is that guy crying? I saw one person who approached me and spoke to me, but I didn't understand, and then I said to him: *Habla español?* Spanish? No, he answered, I don't speak Spanish; I saw the flashing light of a siren turning a corner, and I felt that panic that made me run and hide; I heard myself remind myself that I had killed a policeman, then say: No, no, Marlon, it wasn't you, a car killed him or he killed himself because he decided to run after you; but it wasn't the police that came with the flashing light but rather a street-cleaning truck with water hoses, and I saw how I got everything dirty because I vomited again and again. U espeek Spanish? No, somebody else answered, *mi no habla español*, and even if they did, what could I tell them? While I was running away, I crossed a bridge, and I saw myself crossing many bridges and going past a sign that said QUEEN, and then I looked at the sky and in between the buildings I saw a light and I felt a ray of hope because I thought that somebody was illuminating me; but it wasn't hope or anything like that, just dawn breaking over the city; and I saw the light of day but still nothing familiar, only more people looking at me strangely, probably wondering: Why is that guy shouting? I saw the man who gave me some money I used to buy a doughnut and some coffee, that was all I had enough for. Do u espeek Spanish? *Sí, hablo español,* the cashier said, and I asked him for a doughnut and a cup of coffee and I told him I was lost. Where were you? I don't know. In what part of the city? I don't know. How can I help you? I don't know, I don't know, I don't know. I'm sorry, *amigo*, next please. I saw myself in the street again, walking without stopping until night came and I saw myself surrounded by oil drums and the other street people; again I heard the dull thud of the car hitting the policeman, the policeman hit by the car, and again I saw the bridge and felt the happiness of believing that I was saved and the disappointment at not finding anything besides the same people who were looking at me strangely, wondering: Why is that guy talking to himself? I was talking to God and begging him to hear me, but the only thing I heard was noise in my ears and myself saying: You can tell God never had a mother. From then on I would get lost also in my memories, but there in the shower, as if everything had just happened, I started screaming, stamping on the shit and throwing myself against the walls, maybe trying finally, yes, with one blow, to have the illusion of waking up.

My shouts were so loud that I didn't hear when they opened the door to the bathroom. I just saw huge eyes bulging out of their orbits, and a face that could only have been accompanied by another scream. But that time it wasn't mine.

"Those were my eyes," Giovanny Fonseca said. "Patricia sent me to find out what was going on."

"And he screamed when he saw you," Patricia said.

"I didn't scream," Giovanny protested. "All the screams were yours, Marlon."

The shower was still on and I was curled up in a corner. Giovanny turned off the water and threw a towel over me. Then he knelt down, and looking me straight in the eyes, he said:

"*Tranquilo*, brother, *tranquilo*."

I wish he'd said: You've been dreaming and now it's over. He helped me get up and put on a pair of pants, then he told Patricia that she could come in. She called my name from the door, and for a while she didn't say anything else, but at least she spoke my name, which for someone who's lost is already a ray of light. I suspected that she knew me, and if she knew me, why wouldn't she know Reina? That's why I asked her:

"Do you know Reina?"

"No," she said, "I don't think so."

"She came with me."

"You arrived here alone."

"And Reina?"

"I don't know."

"How did I get here?"

"I don't know that, either."

She came over to me and helped me stand up; when we were out of the bathroom, she said to me:

"My name is Patricia and I'm going to help you. In the meantime, I'm going to bring you something hot to drink."

I obeyed her and nodded in agreement. They say that when she returned, she found me sleeping and still only half dressed; but it's just as well that way, because while she was in the kitchen, Don Pastor, overcome by curiosity, peeked in, and after glancing at me, he exclaimed indignantly:

"Patricia is crazy."

He went over to her and said:

"You're crazy."

Then he left the kitchen hollering, saying what we all say when we come up against a woman's stubbornness, complaining over and over: My wife is crazy. Who can understand her? What, she wants to be canonized? That's how all saints get started, but first they go crazy. And other things like that, things nobody understood, that's what Pastor Gómez shouted.

Not even his shouts woke me up; neither did Patricia's hand shaking my shoulder so that I would drink something hot, not even her "*Despierte, mijo*" or her "*Despierte, Marlon,*" or the sound of the door closing, or the sound of the key turning in the bolt.

Patricia says that I was in a deep sleep and that I hardly moved when she threw a blanket over me and said to me:

"We're going to see what more I can do for you."

The rest was Don Pastor's ongoing complaints, and the commentaries the cooks and the other guys made:

"He's Colombian and he's screwed."

"All Colombians are screwed."

"How long has he been like this?"

"Why don't they just call the cops?"

"No way. I promised him that the police wouldn't come."

"That's one of Saint Patricia's things, and she's crazy."

"It was hard for all of us when we first got here."

The uproar, such as it was, reached the customers, who asked: What's going on? What's the big deal? That's when Pastor Gómez gathered everyone together in the kitchen and, taking his hands out from underneath his poncho so he could use them to emphasize what he was saying, laid down the law: Not one more word about this, because if this gets out, Immigration will come around and then we'll all be screwed.

"And what's more," he added, "that kid is out of here as soon as he can talk."

"And what's more," Patricia interjected, "I want to take advantage of us being here all together to ask you to bring in your extra clothes. Marlon is about your age and size."

"I already told you," Don Pastor interrupted, "just forget that ape is in this place. Focus on your work." Screwing up his mouth and turning his eyes to his wife, he added, "And if any of you ever want someone to one day call you Daddy, keep your eyes on the ball and do your work."

"Don't talk about that boy like that; he deserves respect, too," Patricia protested.

"How do you mean?" Óscar Iván asked, confused. "What he said about our balls or calling him an ape?"

"Enough!" Patricia said.

"He smells like an ape," her husband said.

"And like dirty balls," said Óscar Iván.

The racket that followed was the loudest that restaurant had known in fifteen years, and Pastor Gómez's warnings that tried to reestablish order were totally ineffective. The staff got divided into two gangs: those who supported their boss and those who were with his wife. Every waiter who entered the kitchen was a waiter who gave his opinion, and every empanada that went out was accompanied by some commentary or other, and on and on it went until closing time.

Don Pastor, as usual, was the last to leave. He himself checked to make sure that all the lights, stoves, and ovens were turned off. Next he lowered the grate and checked to make sure it was locked. And whereas before he always took his wife's arm as they walked away together, that night he walked by himself, a few steps behind her, but close enough to say:

"Hopefully tomorrow we'll find something."

But she acted as if she hadn't heard a word. She even reminded the others as they left:

"Don't forget about the clothes."

In the meantime, the one who wasn't me was inside that little room, oblivious to all the commotion outside, maybe because he had enough of his own commotion to deal with. And that guy was in a deep sleep, taking a break from the harshness of New York City, a breather from his mad dash through the labyrinth. There, inside that room, me and the guy who wasn't me were approaching each other; thus was wrought the miracle of Saint Patricia: the coming together of the one who was sleeping and the one who ran out and found himself lost, so that both of them could wake up the next day as one real, whole person.

I think I already said that when I woke up my nightmare got divided into two parts. Waking up didn't bring me the relief dreamers usually feel when they realize, during that short time it takes for them to wake up, that what they thought was reality turns out to be only a bad dream. I didn't have the good fortune to hear those words spoken softly to frightened children at midnight: It's over, it's all right, you were dreaming, but now you are awake.

Anyway, I felt reassured by the idea that nothing could get worse and even a false sense of relief when Patricia showed up and brought me to the kitchen for breakfast and I told her what was going on.

"So you are lost," she said. I nodded, worried, not only because I was admitting it to myself, but also because of the sullen look on that *señor*'s face and his harsh words.

"That *señor* is my husband," Patricia told me, "and his name is Pastor."

"Don Pastor, even if we are in the United States," he insisted from his corner.

Patricia made a face as if she couldn't care less about him, that look women give us men when we are nothing more than furniture. But Pastor Gómez was already at a stage in life when he didn't care about looks, and without taking into account Patricia's efforts, he walked straight over to me. As he approached, I couldn't help wondering what a man dressed like a muleteer, wearing a poncho and a belt pouch and acting like a policeman, was doing in New York City.

"Look, kid," he said, emphasizing his words by wagging his finger, "you've bathed and you've eaten and you're ready to get out of here."

"Pastor!" exclaimed Patricia.

"You already did your thing," he told her. "You already earned your place in heaven; you already gave what you had to give. Now let him get out of here because he's probably got lots of things to do."

"Pastor! This boy is lost," she said facing him, her hands on her waist, her arms sticking out like jug handles to make herself look bigger, even though she was so much shorter than him. Then, more quietly, but with the same strong voice, she said:

"Come on, let's go to the office."

She went ahead of him, gathering up her hair, and he followed, straightening out his poncho. I stayed behind in the kitchen, paralyzed and confused, avoiding the other guys' eyes, though there was one enormous set of eyes I always seemed to meet. Giovanny Fonseca's bulging and encouraging eyes never left me that day, and they made me uncomfortable. At the time, I never suspected that I would soon be seeing through those eyes, that like two beacons, they would help me regain my footing on dry land.

I deduced from the name that Giovanny was Colombian, though afterward he explained that in Italy there are more Giovannys than in Colombia.

"But there are more Johns in Colombia than in the entire United States," he told me.

Slowly he taught me how to make my way along uncertain terrain; he helped me see that there was not only one way but many possible ways of finding Reina.

My mood sank when Patricia and Don Pastor emerged from the office. He went up to the dining room, and she sat down and said to me:

"*Bueno, mijo,* we have to talk."

You could tell she was as nervous as I was, and in her slow, motherly voice, she began talking:

"So, you walked out and couldn't get back."

"Yes, *señora.*"

"Do you know anybody here?"

"No, *señora.*"

"I can't hear you. Talk louder."

"I don't know anybody."

"And you don't remember anything? The building? The street?"

"No, *señora.*"

Patricia took a deep breath and leaned back in her chair. She fingered her apron nervously. The others continued working but slowed down so they could walk casually by us, hoping to catch a piece of our conversation.

"Would you like a cup of coffee?" Patricia asked me.

I said no, thank you. Everything I accepted from them would be just one more excuse to throw me out sooner. She, on the other hand, decided to have coffee.

"There was a sign," I told her.

"What?" She looked up, surprised.

"A big billboard on the building across the street."

The others stood still; suddenly there was no noise of pots and pans clanging or oil sizzling, and one of the cooks had the nerve to ask:

"What did the sign say?"

"Queen," I said.

"Queen or Queens?" Patricia asked.

"Queen. That's *reina* in English, right?"

Nobody answered, but they all looked at each other as if the next guy might be able to give them some kind of explanation. A waiter walked by carrying two plates of food and asked:

"What else did the sign say? What was it?"

"It had other words, but 'queen' was the biggest."

"What did the others say?"

"I don't know. I don't speak English."

There were sighs, snorts, even laughter. Patricia called everybody to order. Then she asked me:

"Do you have a visa?"

"No, *señora*."

"Where did you enter?"

"From Mexico."

"Do you have any money?"

"No, *señora*, nothing."

They brought her coffee; she didn't give it any time to sit on the table and cool off; she picked it up and drank it steaming hot.

"What do you think we should do?" she asked me.

I looked straight at her for the first time. I needed to look in her eyes to see the reflection of my own neediness and confusion.

"I'd like to call home," I told her.

"Colombia?"

I nodded and she held the cup halfway between the saucer and her mouth. She exchanged glances with Giovanny, whose eyes were about to pop out of his head. Everybody else looked at each other. Finally she put the cup down on the table and looked up at the ceiling.

"Let's see, Marlon," she began, "a phone call is something I'll have to discuss. As you know, long-distance calls are very expensive. And, as you probably also know, Pastor doesn't like spending money unless he has to."

She put both hands on the cup but didn't lift it; she turned it around slowly on the saucer.

"It's not that he's a bad person," she continued. "He's really as generous as they come, but he takes good care of what he has, you know, and everything you see here is the result of his work and his diligence. It's all we've got."

I listened to her silently. I didn't have much to say. It was clear that the phone call depended on Don Pastor's mood.

"I think," Patricia continued, "you can stay in that room for tonight. I'll talk to Pastor and then we'll see."

I nodded again without speaking and Patricia sipped her coffee. The others took up their work where they'd left off, and again you could hear the clanging of pots and pans and the crackling of hot oil and the food orders being shouted out and the sounds of constant comings and goings. The excitement and interest in finding out more about the one who was lost quickly passed.

Then, little by little, something happened that still, at that moment, seemed unthinkable: life had to go on.

Reina opened her eyes wide like two saucers and screwed her mouth up as if she was pointing to her father with her puckered lips. Then she spoke loudly so that he would hear, even though it was me she was talking to:

"Come with me outside, Marlon, I'm dying of heat."

But Gonzalo had the television on full blast, so he asked us where we were going only when he saw us get up to leave.

"Out, Papa. We'll be back soon, don't worry."

"Don't go far," Gonzalo said. "This neighborhood is full of drug addicts."

I didn't have the chance to say yes or no, or to ask him what he meant. Reina was pulling on me and only let go when she closed the door to the house.

"What's going on?"

"Come on, let's take a walk to the corner; I don't want my father to hear us."

Reina didn't like that I laughed, so I had to explain:

"I'm not laughing at your father, Reina."

She continued walking, furious.

"You really are something, Reina. I mean, your father doesn't hear us even when we're with him in the dining room."

"But this is a very delicate issue, and you know that when issues are very delicate even the walls start gossiping."

When we reached the corner, Reina cleared up my doubts, or rather, confirmed my suspicions.

"I talked to Fabiola again."

"Okay, go on," I said, "tell me what she told you, tell me what fairy tale she fed you, how she's going to con you."

"Who's talking about conning anybody?! Are you going to let me talk or what?"

I said yes, she could talk. So she leaned against the low wall and pushed herself up so she could sit on the ledge. She tucked the skirt of her school uniform between her legs, which were hanging down over the edge. I stood facing her, my arms crossed over her knees. I smiled at her. I didn't tell her that she looked divine when she was furious. Juancho Tirado had warned me never to say that to a woman because it would only make her more angry. But Carlitos said it was well worth the risk, because the angrier she got, the hotter she got, too, but I never did figure out why Carlitos would want to make a woman he loved angry.

"Fabiola says she can get us in," Reina said.

"Where?"

"Oh, Marlon, cut the shit. The United States!"

"But didn't you say you were going to go to the embassy?"

"Fabiola told me to add up the cost of the trip to Bogotá and all the other travel expenses, and that without papers, they definitely wouldn't give me a visa. That I was just going to waste my time and money."

"And you really want to go?" I asked her.

"Oh, Marlon! I thought we'd already been through this."

I saw she was still furious, so I stroked her thigh, from her knee to the edge of her skirt.

"So, what do we have to do?" I asked her.

"Well, a lot of things," Reina said, her voice getting sweeter. "But first we have to make sure that we agree."

"What does that mean, 'she can get us in'?" I asked her, still caressing her thigh. "How is she going to get us in?"

"She'll explain it all to us. The important thing now is to confirm with her and give her a down payment."

"A down payment?" I stopped stroking.

"Nobody is going to take us for free, not her, not anybody," Reina insisted.

"About how much is this favor going to cost us?"

"About five thousand dollars."

"What?!" I shouted.

"Each," Reina added.

"What?!" I shouted again.

"How much is that in pesos?"

"I don't know," I said, and mechanically began to stroke her thigh again.

"How much is the dollar now?" she asked me.

I shrugged my shoulders and repeated: Ten thousand?! I thought it was such a huge amount of money that we'd never manage to get it, which was actually a relief because that way we wouldn't ever be able to go.

What with one stroke and another, my hand moved up under her skirt, just a little, but enough for Reina to slap my hand.

"No wandering hands," she said.

So I asked her:

"Give me a little kiss, Reina."

But she completely ignored me.

"I'm going to call Fabiola tomorrow."

"Tell her it's too expensive," I suggested.

"Yes," she said; then more to herself than to me, "I'm going to say she can count us in."

"But what about the money?"

"We'll have to get it somehow," she said decisively. Then she suggested, "Come on, come up here."

Thoughtful and worried, I stared at her because at that very moment she decided to smile. She saw how bewildered I was and repeated:

"Come sit down next to me, man," and patted the spot next to her, then added in a sexy voice, "Didn't you say you wanted a little kiss?"

The little kiss turned into a big kiss, the kind you never forget because it was long and juicy and included permission to place my hand under her uniform and freely explore all the parts that, according to what she was whispering in my ear, belonged to me: That's yours, everything's yours, but on condition that we get out of here.

"You want to go to your room?"

"I want to go to the United States, to New York."

The kiss continued with the tongue and the fingers. Then a neighborhood cop rode by on a bicycle and his whistle shattered the moment. The kiss ended with a coy moan from Reina. I licked my damp fingers, wondering if my erection would last until we got to New York.

On the way home we were happy and held hands. I took advantage of the good mood and said to Reina:

"Look, Reina, why don't we keep trying to get a visa? Maybe we'll get lucky and they'll give us one."

"Okay, Marlon," she said, stopping and facing me. "I'm going to ask you some questions, the same ones Fabiola asked me."

"Go on," I said.

"Do you have a credit card?"

"No."

"Do you have a bank account?"

"No."

"Do you have steady work?"

I shook my head.

"Property? A house? A tiny apartment? A car?"

"If only, Reina. What more could I ask for?"

"Okay, next. Do you have an uncle who is a councilman, a senator, or a minister of any damn thing?"

"No, Reina, what's all this about?"

Then she came right up to me, pressed her body against mine, and in a very quiet voice so that nobody could hear, and in a sweetish tone, so as not to offend me, she said:

"You don't have nothing, Marlon."

Then in a louder and stronger voice, so that she and everybody else would know, I said:

"I've got you, Reina."

Then still very quietly and right up against my ear, she answered:

"They won't give you a visa for me."

I was going to say something, maybe a word of protest, but she stuck her finger in my mouth to stop me from talking. She didn't want to hear any arguments that would wake her up from her dream. I had to make do with nibbling on her fingertip.

"My father is watching us."

She pointed with her nibbled finger at one of the windows of the house. There was Gonzalo's silhouette, spreading apart the curtains so he could peek outside. Reina lifted her arm and indicated to him that she was coming.

"I think my father can smell it," she said, standing a bit farther away from me.

"What, you aren't going to tell him?" I asked.

"Are you crazy?!" She had never mentioned her mother, but now she said, "He had enough with my mother."

In a tone I hoped would sound convincing, I said, "The news is going to kill him."

"There won't be any news," she said with much more confidence than I had in my voice.

"It'll kill him anyway."

"It doesn't matter," she said, looking at her father still standing at the window, then added, "because if we stay here, I'll be the one who'll kill myself."

"They told me you haven't gone out for three days and you haven't bathed," Patricia said, standing in the doorway. What did I know about the days or my smell? I'd gotten used to the darkness and my stench, and anyway, what the hell did I care what time it was?

"Here's some more clean clothes. Go take a shower; we're going to call Medellín this afternoon."

Patricia had to repeat it to me:

"Did you hear me? You're going to call home."

At that very moment, I truly believed that all my problems were already solved. It wasn't so hard to talk myself into it. I was sure they knew what had happened to me; Reina would have already told them, or at least Gonzalo, and they would have a phone number for Gloria, her cousin. That's all I could think about as I stood under the shower and scrubbed myself with soap, as if I wasn't just going to talk to them, but I was going to see them, too, and I wanted to be spanking clean. But there was also the other possibility: that I would see her. There was a definite chance I'd see Reina that very night.

Bathed, dressed in clean clothes, and smelling much better, I presented myself to Patricia.

"What a difference, *mijo*."

I smiled. I remember that because it was the first time in a long time I'd smiled. I had lots of reasons, all mistaken of course, but what the hell; in life you've always got to make up reasons to smile.

"*Bueno, mijo*, we're going to call, but first I want to make a few suggestions."

On the other hand, we never have to invent reasons to make our happiness go away. Mostly they come on the heels of a "but."

"The call has to be short, very short. And you have to promise to pay for it when you find work or find somebody, do you understand? You'll work it out with Giovanny later. He's paying for the call."

He was already looking at me when I looked over at him. There were his big eyes. I thought, and I still think, that I'll never be able to repay him, not just for the call that cost a few dollars, but for the gesture. I'll never be able to repay him because things like that don't have a price.

"Come on, then."

I followed Patricia and Giovanny to the office. It was his privilege, in his role as creditor, to be there. Don Pastor, on the other hand, was nowhere to be seen. Patricia put the telephone down in the middle of the desk and offered me the chair.

"The call will be short, but it's still better to talk sitting down."

I obeyed, but when I saw the phone, my fingers cramped up. They clutched the arms of the chair, and I just barely managed to stammer out what I wanted them to do for me.

"You dial, please," I muttered.

"What's the number?"

I said it slowly, taking a breath between numbers.

"It's ringing," she said.

She handed me the phone and I managed to unclench one hand and take it. It was ringing. We all looked at each other. Patricia smiled at me, and Giovanny stared at me with his bulging eyes. Then, over the sound of my own heavy breathing and the pounding of my own heart, I heard Mama's voice on the other end of the line.

"Mama," I said, then felt like crying. I did cry, and I didn't seem to care that I was wasting time or that I had Giovanny standing in front of me with a stopwatch.

There was total confusion on the other end. Mama asked: Marlon? Then she shouted: It's Marlon! Immediately I heard Papa picking up the other extension: Marlon?! Where are you, *hijo*? How are you, Marlon? They took turns firing questions at me without giving me a chance to answer, leaving me only seconds to get a word in edgewise.

Then came the recriminations: Why didn't you tell us? Why did you wait so long to call? We were worried sick. Why did you leave like that? They were fighting with each other to get their questions in, until I could hear that Mama was crying, too. Giovanny Fonseca stood there in front of me, holding up three fingers. Three minutes. They hadn't told me yet what I wanted to hear, so I decided to ask.

"Papa, has Reina been in contact with you?"

Then it came: What are you talking about, *hijo*? What's going on? What, that thief isn't with you?

"Don't call her that, Papa."

And then Mama: But that's what she is. And Papa: What's going on? And Mama: That thief abandoned you, Marlon, didn't she, *mijo*?

"No, Mama, me and Reina lost each other."

And Papa: What are you talking about? And then: Who are you with? Where are you staying? And Mama: I warned you, Marlon, I knew it, I just knew it.

"Papa, I can't talk much. I need you to do me a big favor. I need you to go to her house and find out where she is, get me a phone number for Gloria, her cousin."

Papa said he didn't understand anything, and Mama said I should come home, they were waiting for me.

"I can't, Mama, I've got to find Reina. As soon as you know anything, call me at this number."

While I was giving them the number Patricia had written on a napkin, Papa wanted to know when we had lost each other, and Mama pointed out that it had been such a long time, and it was very strange that nobody had heard from her. Then she said: She's one of those people who never show up because they're lost from the moment they're born. Papa said to me: Anyway, I'm going to see what I can find out.

The second I hung up, Giovanny lowered his arm and put down his watch, but he didn't say a word. Patricia, who'd been fidgeting with her apron during the whole conversation, crossed her arms over her chest and her face turned into a question mark.

"They don't know anything, but they're going to try to find out," I mumbled.

But it was me who had more doubts now, a thousand questions I hadn't even thought of before I'd called. And a thousand possible answers bombarded me along with Patricia's and Giovanny's guesses: Could she be in the same situation as you? But she had someplace to go. Or did she? It's so weird that nobody back home knows anything, unless Immigration got her.

Before they could go on, I stood up, excused myself, thanked them, went to my little room, closed the door, and didn't turn on the light. I couldn't understand why Reina hadn't called to tell them what had happened; and as I tried with a lot of effort to catch my breath, a buzzing began in my ear, as if there was an insect in there that was trying to get out. Then the buzzing started in my other ear, and with both of them buzzing, everything else went blank.

Then that one kind of buzzing got replaced by a different

kind, and I realized I was hearing the very sound that can kill a person who has been condemned to wait: the ringing of a telephone. I waited for somebody to knock and say: Marlon, you've got a call, it's your father. But nobody came to get me, and that ringing just stirred up the other buzzing, and they all joined together to make a concert in my ear.

At some point everybody left, without saying good-bye or locking up. Not even Patricia showed her face. But what did I care about niceties or freedom at that moment? Later, I cared a lot when the telephone rang in the middle of the night, and this time it was my father's voice on the line.

"Bad news, *hijo*."

"What?"

"Nobody has heard from her."

"That can't be."

"They still think she's with you."

"She must be with her cousin. Did you get the number for me?"

"Gonzalo says this Gloria person is not her cousin, that she must be a friend, or who knows what. All of Reina's cousins live here."

"Are you sure, Papa?"

"At least that's what he told me."

"So?"

"So come on back here and stop playing around."

I should have said to him: Nobody is playing, Papa, this is serious, so serious that there is no way I can go back without Reina.

"We'll see, Papa."

"It'll cost me an arm and a leg while you're trying to decide, *hijo*. So we'll call you back later."

Obviously, it didn't turn out as I'd expected, that this whole mess would get cleared up with one phone call. Just the opposite—everything was only just beginning. But before I was able to reach this conclusion, I had to curse everything and kick the wall all night long. The kicks didn't have much effect because my fate was already sealed, and to make sure I didn't forget, Giovanny took it upon himself to spell it out for me:

"I'm not sure if it's you or her who's lost. But as long as you stay shut up in this room, you're never going to find her. If you're planning on staying in this country, you'd better go out and find yourself some work and a place to live. I can help you, but you've also got to help yourself. So as soon as you make up your mind, let's start at the beginning."

That's how he explained it to me on the fifth day of my being shut in, by which time I didn't even want to talk to my parents. As soon as they'd tell me they hadn't heard any news about Reina, I'd tell them I had to hang up and I'd go back to my cell.

"So what's the beginning?" I asked Giovanny.

"Come on out, come take a walk with me."

"I can't, Giovanny."

"Here, the people who say that, they go straight to hell." Then he repeated, "Come take a walk with me."

We went outside, him in front and me a few steps behind, just like when I used to walk with her. But it wasn't just a walk, as Giovanny said, it was a swim through a current of human beings, and it took me a lot of effort not to drown in the waves.

"There's a lot of people," I said.

"This is nothing," Giovanny Fonseca said.

We rushed down some stairs into a tunnel where there was more noise and more people.

"These are the intestines of the beast," he told me. But before I could understand or ask him to explain, I heard a roar and then a train came. Giovanny pushed me ahead of him into the car, but it was so crowded, we got separated. I didn't take my eyes off Giovanny Fonseca for a second. The train swayed and shook, and he pointed to the overhead bar to tell me to grab on to it. I got up the courage and looked at the people around me, and they all kind of looked like me, which made me wonder: Where am I? There aren't any gringos here.

Giovanny grabbed me and led me out to the street; he started walking fast and pointing to things and naming them, but to me it was like he was talking in English. We stopped in front of an old building with an iron staircase that zigzagged its way up the outside of the building. "Now, *hermano*, start climbing," he said.

"What are you talking about?"

"Follow me."

I watched him go up, saw him climbing with his hands and feet, using the rails and the bars. Come on, he said, and I thought: I can't, but it was clear that I couldn't not be able to. So I tried, and while I was climbing, I thought: If I can do this, I can do anything. And among those things I knew I could do was find Reina. So I braved the stairs and with my final breath I reached Giovanny, who was waiting for me at the top. We perched ourselves on the roof under some enormous letters that began to light up. Everything looked so tiny down below. It was getting dark and the wind was pushing against us.

"Look," Giovanny said, and he pointed to a flock of birds flying on our left. Then he turned around and pointed in front of us. I hadn't seen her, nor had I heard her growl, but there she was.

"Take a good look," he told me. "That's the beast you've got to tame."

In front of me was New York City, magnificent and challenging, welcoming and disproportionate. Like a gigantic and overcrowded chessboard.

It's a long bus ride. Miami is way down there, all the way at the other end. I didn't expect to see much along the way. And I'm not particularly surprised by a landscape infested with gigantic *M*s of McDonald's, and the just-as-big plastic shells of Shell, but I do feel unnerved by the suicidal crows that dash across the freeways. Then I see some crosses decorated with flowers along the side of the road. I only see two or three of them and keep looking for more, but don't find any; in my country they're everywhere, at every spot where at least one person has died, around every curve, because our roads seem to be built with the intention of killing us, and all that's left are those crosses along the side of the road, the only witnesses to the people who went flying or rolling, a shoe here or there—there always seems to be a lost shoe wherever there's been a tragic death—to tell us if the person who passed on was a man, a woman, or a child. But we don't have crows or freeways, so we have to make do with dogs run over in the middle of the street and once in a while a dead burro, or whatever is left of him after the vultures have done their job.

So while everybody else is sleeping, I look for crosses decorated with flowers and scenery that passes by and doesn't bring any other surprises. Occasionally there's a fire and a big uproar, trucks and people trying to put it out. And signs and more signs announcing the approach of cities that we leave behind without ever seeing. Charlotte got off in one of those cities and left behind a seat covered with blueberry muffin crumbs. Everybody is sleeping, and I don't understand how they can with their knees crammed in and aching.

I keep thinking about her. The day I stop thinking about Reina will be the day it rains upward, from the earth to the sky. What can a lost man think about other than the only place he remembers? And Reina, Queen, Queen Reina, Queens, is also that place where I left her alone and that sign that is the only thing I remember.

She had her fixed ideas, or maybe she just had that one that always faced north, the same direction she'd face when she'd stand and watch the airplanes flying overhead, when she'd follow them with her eyes while she sighed or mumbled a question under her breath, so quiet that she could barely hear it herself: Where could the airplanes be going? She'd only stop looking when the clouds swallowed them up; then she'd take a nosedive and get into a foul mood. It was always better not to talk to her when she was on the rebound from a dream. Nobody else knew this, only me, because I was told off so many times for just asking: What's wrong, Reina? And she'd answer: What? Does something always have to be wrong or what?

My friends told me: That happens to you because you're an idiot, because you should never ask a woman what's wrong when you think something's wrong. Why? I asked them, and they explained to me: Because what's wrong with them almost always has something to do with you and it's almost never anything good.

But I did want to know what was wrong and what she was

thinking about, especially at the beginning, because later I would learn to read her different-colored eyes and the expressions on her face. It was easy to understand her staring at the airplanes and that big sigh she let out when she couldn't see them anymore. It was easy to understand that she wanted to leave. We all wanted to leave; it's better to be far away than dead or kidnapped or living in poverty. But it wasn't so easy to understand her "Let's just kill ourselves" or her "Just kill yourself and leave me alone," because this had more to do with her own self than our murderous country. Just like her eyes following those airplanes, her "Let's just kill ourselves" also showed a deep longing for something. And there was that one time she made good on her word.

"Reina won't open the door." Gonzalo called me very early one morning.

He'd been knocking for a while and she hadn't answered. And the key? She has the key, he told me; you know how willful she is.

"I'm on my way."

She didn't open for me, either; she didn't respond at all. Gonzalo was trembling. You know how she is, he told me, the strange ideas she has.

"Reina, open the door! Reina, open it!"

Gonzalo was referring either to her suicide threats or the questions she always asked herself about life. Two days before, a homeless person had approached us, a bum asking for money, and Reina had lost control; she began to insult him and tell him to go kill himself, that he should disappear, that he shouldn't exist. Then she cried for a while, but when she calmed down, she asked me: What's it all about, Marlon? To live or to be alive?

"Reina, open the door, please!"

Gonzalo and I threw all our weight against the door and on the third try we crashed through, door and all. From where we landed on the floor, we saw her lying on the bed with one leg hanging out from under the covers. We shook her, sat her up, talked to her; we begged her to respond.

"Get the car out, Gonzalo, we've got to get her to the hospital."

I drove and he held her in his arms as if she was Christ just taken down from the cross. She was breathing but she'd lost all her color and warmth. Gonzalo was also pale, and I was frozen.

While they were flushing out her insides and getting ready to return her to us, I told Gonzalo about what happened with the street person, even though I knew that this wasn't really what had made Reina carry out her threats. It was New York and the frustration of not yet getting the money we needed to go that made her take the pills. Luckily, they were only a few, the doctor said, but anyway we had to watch over her and not leave her alone.

That's the reason—because she was alone in New York City—that I decided to stay and tame the beast.

"Don't take this business about taming the beast too seriously," Giovanny warned me when I told him what I meant to do. "I mean," he added, "you can't do it by force; you've got to use skill, and don't ever start thinking you're so clever, because they're always one step ahead of us: by the time we're just getting going, they're already on their way back."

I listened carefully to the instructions given to me by Giovanny Fonseca, twenty-eight years old, who has lived in the United States for five years, illegal, broke, but in spite of it all, married and with three children. The only thing he's missing is a dog, like in Colombia, where in addition to feeding all those hungry mouths, they've got to leave the scraps for the pet.

"Here, our aboriginal cunning doesn't cut it," he continued.

"It doesn't there, either."

"But even less here. Here what works best is observing: you've got to watch and follow, watch and imitate, and obey, even if you think nobody is watching, because somebody always is."

"Like at school," I interrupted him.

Giovanny took a deep breath and opened his eyes so wide I thought they were going to pop out of his head. Then he said to me as if he was scolding me:

"Just look at everything that happened to you because you threw a cigarette butt on the sidewalk."

"It wasn't only because of the butt," I protested, "but also because of fear."

"But if you hadn't thrown it in the street . . ." Giovanny Fonseca's eyes bulged.

"Yeah, but if I hadn't run away . . ."

"A goddamn cigarette butt," Giovanny repeated.

We looked at each other as if to say: So who's right here? But Giovanny always won when it came to staredowns, so I bowed my head.

"Here, what's worth fighting for," he said, "is to make even a tiny part of the dream that brought us here come true."

"Reina brought me here."

"Forget about Reina," he told me, and I thought: When it rains upward or when the sun rises in the west. That's why I asked him:

"What is it I've got to do, Giovanny?"

"For starters, *hermano*, you need to work."

"What is it I've got to do to forget about her?" I insisted.

Giovanny threw back his head, crossed his hands behind his head, and said without any ifs, ands, or buts:

"This is a problem." He stated it emphatically, switching to English.

Nothing worked. Not habit, not routine, not the passing of time, not even the bright idea of replacing Reina with another love. Not even New York City could do it, with all its speed and seduction, with its own way of measuring time, its shorter hours so that everything seems so unreal, so that every time you look at your watch it's always too late and you've got to run to get there; here, everybody's running. But who am I to talk, me who started off in this city running?

It was very hard to come out of my shell. Slowly I expanded my territory a few steps at a time: from the room to the tiny bathroom, from there to the kitchen, from the door to the sidewalk, and from there to the corner. Later, little by little, I got to the next block, then to the following one, then finally to the old building and its rooftop where Giovanny had taken me to show me the beast that was rising out of the water: Manhattan in all its monstrosity and the silhouette of its tentacles at sunset. You never really get used to its presence. When we saw it the first time, I was in shock and Reina was quivering with excitement. It suddenly appeared in front of the bus that was bringing us from San Antonio. I was dozing off and I felt her grab my hand. Look, she said, trying to catch her breath, and for a moment I didn't understand how there could be more lights on earth than in the heavens, but then Reina confirmed it: It's New York City; and then she repeated in a quieter voice: My New York. With my mouth hanging open, I looked around at the promissory landscape of twinkling lights and skyscrapers.

"This city has its own rules," everybody told me.

"And where are the instructions?" I asked them.

"They're the same ones you were born with."

Cheap philosophy, I thought, sitting on the rooftop looking out at Manhattan. To think there was a time I wanted to study philosophy, the real stuff. And how when I told Reina, she thought that was so funny.

"I still haven't decided," I said.

"Between what and what?" she asked me.

"Between studying engineering or philosophy and humanities."

"You're worse than that woman who can't decide."

"Which woman?"

"The one who doesn't know whether to eat a *buñuelo* or go to New York."

Reina burst out laughing, then said:

"I've decided: I'm going to New York," and then she added, "I'm hungry, Marlon."

I invited her for some *buñuelos*. On the way, she asked me:

"What do your parents say about it?"

"My father says the decision is easy. If I want to eat food, I'll study engineering; if I want to eat shit, I'll study the other. Can you imagine, he doesn't even call it by its name, he just refers to it as 'the other.'"

Reina looked away from me and stared at her *buñuelos*. Before taking her first bite, she asked me, "What do you think?"

What was I supposed to say to her? She was more interested in that *buñuelo* than listening to me, so I said, "The decision isn't as simple as my father wants to make it."

In any case I applied to both majors and didn't get into either. Again life was deciding for me, but Reina didn't agree.

"What life, whose life, what are you talking about?!" she said furiously. "Don't blame life! Blame this country and the assholes who run it. Or let's see," she continued angrily, "you tell me: in what respectable country do they just not let you study?"

"Calm down, Reina."

"Only in a country of monsters!"

Her temper would rise, she'd explode, and a minute later she'd calm down. She'd cross her arms and sigh; then, in a calm voice, she'd begin by saying: We should go, let's just go, Marlon, let's get out of here. Just like that, like our country was a boring party, or like we were walking out in the middle of a dull circus performance.

Illuminated by my memories and the light from the huge letters I was leaning against, I thought about all this and more on that rooftop facing Manhattan. Until finally one afternoon, drowning in memories, I started wondering if I was going to keep living off charity, off scraps from the Tierra Colombiana, off cold empanadas and old memories. If I carried on like this, I might as well go back home: I wasn't gaining anything by airing out my problems on a rooftop.

Go back? I asked myself; and then I said to myself: I'll stay wherever Reina is, and I know that she's here, somewhere down there, even if I can't see her. Reina is not one to betray her own dreams.

How are we going to get that money, Reina?"

"Well, there are only three ways," she said. "Working, gambling, or stealing."

"Out of those three, there's only one that's possible for us."

"Right," she said. "Stealing."

I let out a laugh and had a mind to say to her: That's a good joke, Reina. But since I wasn't sure she had meant it that way, I didn't say anything and just kept laughing until I had enough time to process the possibility that Reina actually meant what she said.

"How about we ask for a loan?" I suggested.

"From who?"

I went over a short list in my head, a pathetic, naive, and very short list that gave me only a stupid grin to tack onto my face, an answer that didn't convince Reina at all.

"How about we apply for a scholarship?" I tried again.

Reina sighed impatiently. She didn't seem much interested in looking for alternatives. Her decision had already firmly taken root and she opened her mouth only to confirm it further: I'm going there to work, earn dollars, get ahead, have a child. And I don't think a scholarship is going to help me do that.

"A child?" I asked, frightened.

"Yes," she said. "A girl."

"But Reina . . ."

She smiled at me. She stared at my mouth, like she was wondering whether it was worth it to give me a kiss. So I aimed for her lips, wondering if it would be worth it to follow them, and the answer was yes, it would definitely be worth it.

"And the money?" I asked again.

"We'll have to get it somehow," she answered as usual.

"Seriously, Reina, what are you going to do? Rob a bank?"

"What are you talking about?" she said. "I don't even own a pistol."

That night, I let the cat out of the bag with my friends. We were outside, on the corner of my block, sitting on the curb. I told them:

"Hey, you guys, it looks like I'm outta here."

"See you tomorrow, Marlon," said Carlitos.

"No," I clarified. "I mean I'm going to New York."

The three shouted in chorus:

"What?! When?!"

"This is top secret," I warned them. "Reina will kill me if she knows you know."

"With Reina?!"

"With who do you think?" I answered.

"With your mommy and daddy?" Montoya said.

"Be careful," I warned again. "They don't know, either."

"So you're not just going away," Juancho said. "You're running away."

"Well . . ."

They all looked at each other, and while they were looking at each other, I noticed that they looked worried, and to tell the truth, sad. We'd never considered the possibility of one of us going away. Not so soon, anyway.

"And the visa?" asked Carlitos.

"Well, there's a woman who's going to help us."

"What, get you the visa?" Carlitos insisted, insinuating something other than that he was simply curious.

"No," I told them, "they're not going to give us one."

Carlitos stood up—breaking the circle—and walked a few steps away from us. Montoya and Tirado looked at each other again.

"Everything's going to be all right," I said, trying to smooth things over.

Carlitos remained a ways away with his hands in his pockets, looking farther into the distance. The three of us, still sitting on the curb, passed around a cigarette without talking until Carlitos, behind us, said:

"See you tomorrow."

We watched him walk away, his hands still dug into his pockets, until he disappeared around the corner. Then Juancho Tirado said:

"It's because of his brother."

"You remember," Eduardo said to me.

"He got killed crossing the border," Juancho added.

"And his wife disappeared," Eduardo said.

They looked me right in the eye as they spoke, and the expressions on their faces changed from concern to a warning. They didn't pass me the cigarette again.

"Well, there are also lots of folks who get across," I told them.

"And others they send back," Juancho said.

"And others that never come back," said Eduardo.

Montoya offered what was left of the cigarette to Juancho, but he didn't want it. Montoya didn't want to smoke, either, even though there were a few drags left. He flicked it away over my shoulder. I said to them:

"Everything depends on how things are done."

"And you are going to do things right, of course," Juancho Tirado said.

"Of course."

"Ohhh," said Montoya, and he looked over at Tirado, who screwed up his mouth.

Eduardo stood up, brushed the dust off his rear end, and said: Okay, I guess we'll see each other tomorrow; and he left without offering any further commentary. Juancho and I stayed there sitting on the curb.

"Keep your foot still," Juancho told me. I hadn't realized it was shaking. The air was heavy and it was very hot.

"How much are they charging you?" Juancho asked.

"We still don't know. We'll find out soon."

The lie made sweat bead up on my forehead, and my foot began to shake again.

"And the money, where are you going to get it?"

"We'll have to get it somewhere," I said to him, just like Reina had said to me.

Again Juancho Tirado said: Ohhh. And just as I was changing the position of my foot, he stood up, brushed off his pants, and gave me a pat on the shoulder.

"See you tomorrow, *hermano*." He turned around and walked away.

As soon as I could, I also stood up and walked away, keeping my eyes down, like Carlitos; the difference was that he had his brother in his head and I had Reina, and he was probably thinking affectionately about his brother, and for the first time I was feeling something else toward her. Something she suspected that night, because when I called her, like I did every night before we went to sleep, she complained:

"Today you haven't told me that you love me."

Yes, I was loving her, but with a different flavor, or I was loving her with fear, and it's more difficult to love that way. Anyway, I said to her:

"Why should I tell you if you already know?"

"So do me a favor and remind me."

She said it in a voice that didn't make me want to say "I love you," but I said it anyway:

"I love you, Reina."

"How much?" she asked irritably.

"Up to the sky," I answered, almost mockingly. The silence that followed was only broken by both our breathing. Until she said:

"I'll be happy if you love me until we get to New York," and she hung up the phone.

I stayed where I was, lying on my bed, looking up at the ceiling, the phone buzzing against my chest. There was only one thought churning in my head—the possibility of saying to Reina: I'm not going.

That night I had two dreams. In the first one, Reina was laughing her head off and she said to me: I'm going to kill myself; in the second, I dreamed I was shitting fish. I'd dreamed the first one before, and it always scared me, but this was the first time I'd ever dreamed the second one. I decided to use it as an excuse to call Reina the next morning so I could tell her about it.

"You were in such a weird mood last night, it's no wonder you had strange dreams," she said, not very enthusiastically.

"I was just tired."

"Tired?" she asked. "Of what?"

My dream hadn't been a very good pretext and Reina kept going on in the same vein. She sounded like now it wasn't a question of whether I would decide to go, but whether she would decide to take me. But she did ask:

"What kind of fish were they?"

"Orangish," I said. "And they looked like ballerinas."

"And what were they doing?"

"Swimming around in the toilet bowl."

"Did you flush?"

"No," I said, "that's when I woke up."

"What a weird dream."

"Could it mean something?" I asked.

Reina was silent, maybe thinking deeply about it. Then she said:

“Maybe that everything inside us isn’t shit?”

Reina had, in addition to different-colored eyes, a very unusual prism she saw life through. And after a while I understood that it was because of this prism, and not her bicolor eyes, that I followed her.

"The last one here cleans the bathrooms."

This wasn't some kind of child's dare; it was one of the laws of immigration. And like every self-respecting law, it doesn't apply to everybody, only those who have the bad luck to have it applied to them. I was one of those. I didn't even have the right to consider it part and parcel of my bad fortune; on the contrary, I was expected to view it as a privilege. They even congratulated me for finding work.

"This calls for a celebration," Giovanny Fonseca managed to say.

The truth is, it took a lot of effort to get them to give me the job. It took Patricia more than a week to soften up Don Pastor, because every time she looked at him, he said: No, no, and no again. Before she could even open her mouth to say something, he had already shouted his "No, no, and no again." Apparently she was sleeping in a different room and wearing her hair up, she was using the formal *usted* when she talked to him, she didn't go with him to their tango classes, she refused to say hello to him, and finally she brought out the ultimate weapon: she nagged him. Not caring whether her husband was paying attention or not, she sharpened her tongue, warmed up her vocal cords, and delivered her monologues. But Don Pastor carried on completely unfazed: he gave orders, took orders, and talked to other people as if Patricia was a radio that somebody had forgotten to turn off. She kept saying angrily that she was going back to Colombia, that she was hereby turning the United States over to people who had become cold and unfeeling—she said this loudly and in front of her husband—and that everybody here got amnesia and forgot their roots and their values.

"The day after tomorrow I'm going back to Colombia," she said one morning. "I'm going where there are people who still listen and care."

That's when Pastor Gómez answered her for the first time, giving her an ironic smile that made her even more upset and angry.

"I guess you haven't been listening to the news recently," he said to her, "because they're worse there than here. Maybe you should look around for another country."

Patricia picked up the telephone, dialed, and even I heard her say: Thank you, ma'am, I'd like to reconfirm—with the emphasis on "re"—my reservation for Medellín for tomorrow. And then in a louder voice she said: In first class. Don Pastor let out a shout that could be heard in the dining room upstairs and made all of us run wildly around in different directions. I went and shut myself up in my cell. I didn't even have to plug my ears not to hear what they were saying, because anyway I felt so dizzy I couldn't listen. At that moment, I would have done anything in the world to be somewhere, anywhere, else, anywhere else and at any other time; I don't think I'd ever felt so strongly that I was in the wrong place and at the wrong time.

The next day Patricia arrived with a suitcase and looking very happy. We were all sad, though, because we thought she was actually going to carry out her threat and leave us, and once again I pictured myself lost, without the only person who would care what happened to me. She arrived alone in a taxi, not a sign of Don Pastor anywhere. Some of them said to her: Think again about what you are doing, Patricia; please don't go, Patricia, you know, this restaurant, without you . . .

"No, no," she explained, "this suitcase isn't for me."

Then we all looked at each other, thinking that the suitcase was for Don Pastor, that he was the one leaving, something that happens a lot in marriages, the "You go or I go" syndrome. But that's not what it was this time. The suitcase, it turned out, was for me. I was the one who was leaving, but what I understood least of all was how happy Patricia seemed. I even thought I saw the dark face of betrayal.

"I had to negotiate, *mijo*," Patricia told me. "Tit for tat."

She invited me to sit down and talk. She explained the agreement she had reached with her husband.

"We've all got to give in a little. That's what compromises are all about."

She told me: You leave but you stay. But since this was impossible to understand, she added: You stay here to work, but you go live somewhere else. I heard some clapping. It was Giovanny Fonseca in the background. Anyway, I still didn't understand. What do you mean? Live where? Work? But where will I live?

"One step at a time, *mijo*."

She repeated to me what she had told Don Pastor: He's staying but he's leaving. They were offering me the great opportunity to work: You'll start the same place everybody else starts; then, more gently: You'll start in the bathrooms.

"We've got to celebrate," proposed Giovanny, who was still standing in the background.

But not only that: We can't pay you what we pay everybody else, maybe a little less, but you'll get by. I couldn't see the expression on my face, but now I can imagine it. All of a sudden it must have become the face of somebody who cleans toilets, a face full of piss and shit, doubtful and resigned, maybe from trying to pretend he doesn't see or is resigned to his fate of having to clean up the hairs that sneak around the edges of the urinal, or the phlegm some filthy slob leaves in the sink.

I was someone who barely and with a lot of scruples wiped myself clean of my own shit; who gagged whenever he saw somebody else's shit when they'd forgotten to flush the toilet; who could only take a shit in my own house, or if I really had to go, at Reina's, then soaked the bathroom in perfume afterward; who learned to piss with perfect aim so I wouldn't spray the edges of the toilet bowl, and if by chance a few drops did spill on the edge, I'd wipe them off immediately with toilet paper; and who sometimes even cleaned the edge that somebody else had sprayed so whoever used the bathroom after me wouldn't think I had been the culprit. This same me, for God's sake, was going to clean bathrooms.

The first thing I asked myself was whether it was worth staying in this country not only to eat shit but to clean it as well. And even worse, other people's shit. I wondered if it was worth doing for Reina's sake. As usual, whenever I thought about it, the answer was the same: It's worth cleaning shit, eating shit, even blessing shit; because even at that moment, just like every day before, I imagined myself back home, in my country, in Medellín, and in my house, in my room with my things, my friends, living comfortably with Papa and Mama. I imagined myself sitting there surrounded by everything and without her. And I saw myself as incomplete, missing an arm, with only a leg and a half, half blind, as if I had stepped on a mine like the ones they bury in our fields; I saw myself grumpy and even going bald, and sad, as sad as I am now remembering how I felt when I chose shit over returning.

"When can I start?" I asked Patricia with a generous smile, as if the work really was a gift she was giving me.

She answered, "Today, *mijo*, why wait?"

"Where am I going to live?" And that's as long as Patricia's smile lasted. She cleared her throat and said: Today I'm going to find you a place to stay. Then she smiled again, and even me, who was so grateful to her, even I couldn't help but see something in her smile that reminded me of Fabiola's.

"It'll be five thousand dollars each," Fabiola said, smiling as usual and as if she was awarding us that money instead of getting it from us.

"How long do we have?" Reina asked, excited.

"I'm not the one who's so eager to go," she said sarcastically. "Just give me the money when you want to go. On the other hand," Fabiola added, "I suggest you don't wait too long; the dollar is going up, you know, and these people raise their prices when it does."

We were in a café, not Fabiola's office. That's why she spoke so confidently and smiled so widely, not caring about the cheese bits that were stuck between her teeth. I'm sure that woman was smiling because she was thinking about the dollars she would get out of us, while Reina lowered her head and I silently pleaded with her: Why don't you just give it up, Reina? We can stay here and still do everything you wanted to do there.

"Don't worry," Reina said to her, still avoiding her eyes, "we're going to get the money."

"Okay, just let me know," Fabiola said, knowing she had won. "And of course, don't even think of calling me at the office."

She didn't pay for the sandwich she had eaten or the coffee. She got up, stamped a couple of cheap, perfumed kisses on our cheeks, and walked away cheerfully, clicking her tongue against her teeth.

I toyed with the saltshaker while I waited for Reina to say something. But she didn't say anything except to tell me to ask for the check. I took out my wallet and felt like asking her if that woman was going to deduct the price of her food from what we owed her. Maybe we could just pay for the trip with snacks. But I knew that Reina wouldn't want to hear my comments, so I shut up and paid without making a fuss.

At the bus stop Reina told me: We have to find the money. I pretended to be staring at something far away, trying to read the number on the bus that was coming toward us.

"Here it comes," I told her.

"You're playing the fool," Reina told me.

"I heard you perfectly."

"So?"

"That's ten thousand dollars, Reina."

"And?"

"We'll never get that kind of money. We're staying here."

"I already told you, Marlon: I'll die first. And I'm not going to say it again."

I haven't had that amount of money at one time the whole time I've been here, and I doubt if I ever will. Everything I've earned, the little I've earned, I've spent on looking for her. Money down the drain because I spent most of it on false scents; the only real one didn't cost a penny. Well, not completely: this trip has a price, and going back to being with Reina is going to cost me even more.

Here you are,” Patricia said, and she handed me my work tools: a bucket, gloves, soap, a mop, a broom, rags, and rubber boots. I thought: The bucket must be to vomit in, the soap to wash myself, the rags to wipe away my tears, and the broom to fly away with.

“Everything must always be spotlessly clean,” Patricia said. “Impeccable.”

I thought: Yes, of course, if shit was transparent, and women didn’t leave their menstrual blood, and men didn’t leave spit wads, and if everybody pissed, like me, into the center of the bowl.

“Every time somebody goes in, you have to go in after them and clean up.”

I have to look them in the eyes, find out who the proud owner of what I’m cleaning up is; listen to the sounds they make, get to know the owner of the trickle, the flood, the farts, and the phlegm; tell the next person: You may go in now, I’ve cleaned up what the other left, now it’s your turn to get it dirty.

“We’ll also need you in the kitchen,” Patricia continued. “It gets pretty filthy in there.”

There's filth everywhere, because that is what we are: filthy slobs who always have shit inside just waiting for the intestines' orders to let it out. And the order strikes without warning and in the least expected places, like in a restaurant, for instance. But not to worry: There will always be somebody to deal with anonymous shit.

"You have to clean the food off the plates and silverware, throw it into bags, and take out the garbage."

I will participate in the entire process, dealing with everything that is thrown out before it goes into the mouth and afterward.

"It's easy work," Patricia told me, "and you'll make enough to live on."

"Yes, *señora*."

"Are you pleased?"

"Of course."

I remembered Reina and looked over at the toilets, determined to face them head-on. I told myself: After all is said and done, it's only shit. Then I looked at Patricia and said:

"Thank you for this opportunity."

The first hour, there wasn't much action. The job didn't seem so complicated. Two or three women came in to pee, another employee and a client did the same; until then, only liquid results. The only thing that made me uncomfortable was being in such close quarters. I'd spent all night and all morning in that basement, and I began to feel like I needed some fresh air. I even felt like having a smoke; since that fateful day, I hadn't lit a cigarette. I didn't have any left. It was because of my very last one that I had gone running off.

Giovanny came downstairs to go to the bathroom and put on his Colombian cowboy outfit, the one they hoped would make the restaurant more exotic. Before going in, he asked me how I was doing: *Cómo vas,* bro?

"Hanging in there."

"Earning *dolares*, eh?"

I still hadn't seen a greenback. I could barely remember the ones we had when we arrived, the ones that had disappeared so quickly. With each dollar we spent, a little piece of ourselves—the little we had brought with us—had also disappeared, until there was nothing left; and without money we were nobody.

"Giovanny," I called to him before he went into the bathroom.

"What?"

"Nothing."

While I waited for him to come out, I plucked up the courage to ask him something that with my friends back home was part of saying hi to each other. Sometimes we didn't even have to ask for it: it was just offered around, or all it took was the simple movement of holding up two fingers as if you were holding an invisible cigarette. I hadn't seen Giovanny smoking, but maybe he could get me a cigarette from somebody else.

"Giovanny," I said to him when he came out of the bathroom in his costume, "do you have a cigarette?"

He opened the bag he carried his clothes in and took out a pack. I actually felt excited.

"Take two," he said.

"Do you have a light?"

He knocked the cigarette out of my mouth and opened his eyes to a supernatural size.

"Don't even think of it."

"What?" I asked, horrified.

"Smoking inside," he explained to me. "Here you only smoke outside, even if it's raining, storming, snowing, or there's thunder and lightning."

He suggested we go outside; he told me it was a beautiful day, and I mentioned to him that I hadn't been outside since the day before. He said we should take the opportunity to have a smoke before it got real busy, because then we wouldn't have a minute until the evening.

"And Don Pastor?" I asked him. "You think he'll let me?"

"He's counting money," Giovanny said. "The world could blow up and he wouldn't notice."

I was able to confirm Giovanny's statement when we walked right past him and he didn't even look up. He was counting to himself, silent and happy, moistening his fingers with his spit so he wouldn't miss a single bill. Outside, the sun was shining and it was the warmest day yet since I'd arrived. Giovanny lit first my cigarette, then his. I inhaled with a sense of purpose and a certain amount of fear. I hadn't smoked since that night, and I thought I didn't deserve to ever smoke again for the rest of my life, but I also thought that it was time to treat myself to this first and brief pleasure. I was really enjoying that cigarette. Giovanny noticed how I was feeling it right down to my bones.

"Tastes good, doesn't it, brother?"

I nodded as I took another puff and looked around.

"What's this called?" I asked.

"What?"

"This street."

"Roosevelt Avenue."

It was inconceivable to me that a street where the only things you could see were signs in Spanish would have a name in English, where *vallenatos*, *merengues*, and *rancheras* poured out of car radios, hair salons, and record stores full blast. It didn't take much effort to make believe you were on a street in downtown Bogotá or Medellín.

"This doesn't look like the United States," I commented to Giovanny.

"This is more the United States than anywhere else is," he said.

This was difficult to understand, but later I figured it out. It's not that New York was more the United States than anywhere else was, but it was also the world. And there I was in that piece of the world that had been assigned to me, bombarded from all sides by my music, my language, by people who looked just like me; but without a place to stay.

"Giovanny, where am I going to live?"

He had been smoking his cigarette without looking at me once, but now he turned his bulging eyes on me and told me something that I didn't manage to hear because at that very moment a train passed right overhead. I saw him moving his mouth and looking at me with a certain amount of concern on his face while the street shook and the metallic structure that held up the subway rattled. I wanted to say: Repeat that, Giovanny, I didn't hear anything; but before the train had passed, I watched him toss the butt on the ground. My blood ran cold, and again I felt like running.

"Time to get back inside," he told me.

I waited, terrified, for the police to arrive, but nobody appeared and nobody seemed to care that Giovanny had just tossed a cigarette butt on the sidewalk. That's when I knew for sure that the cigarette butt didn't have anything to do with whatever the policeman wanted to talk to me about. Even so, I rushed inside like a rat scurrying into his cave.

I found Patricia in the kitchen and asked her:

"Where am I going to live, Patricia?"

She turned toward me, looked me up and down, and said:

"*Caramba, mijo*, your work is exemplary!"

She continued with her chores, helping with lunch prep. Everybody was rushing around, talking to each other but not stopping to look at anybody. The only one who looked at me was Pastor Gómez; he had come down to check out what was going on in the kitchen. I moved off to the side when I felt him staring at me with those eyes that seemed to be saying: Go to hell, Marlon Cruz. I put on my gloves and got my equipment ready so that when Don Pastor came out of the kitchen he would see that I was ready to get to work. But when he came out, he didn't see me; he was arranging his poncho, his belt, and his machete, which I never doubted he'd use if I didn't do a good job. I stood there wondering what the gringos made of Don Pastor and where the hell I was going to live.

All this happened on my first day of work, though I didn't think any of it was very important because I expected Reina to appear at any moment, and then I would take off with her. That's what I told my parents, anyway, when they called me early in the morning.

"Today I'm starting work."

"Finally, *hijo*. Doing what?"

I'd already worked it out to give them an answer that wouldn't hurt them so much.

"Well, as a waiter, like everybody here."

Like everybody who had left home and ended up cleaning toilets, but who lied and talked about how well they were doing, all their triumphs, how they were living the gringo dream; when the fact was, even if we had a job and the opportunity to fondle a few dollars before they were sucked away, spent on basic necessities, we were much worse off than when we left, because in addition to everything else, we felt lonely, we were alone, shipwrecked in the middle of New York City.

"Don't you want to reconsider and just come home?"

"What for, Mama? I'm going to be fine here."

"And they'll pay you?"

"Of course, Papa."

Papa asked because he had worked for nothing half his own life. And the other half, he'd been poorly paid, but that shouldn't come as a surprise: in a country where life has so little value, work has even less.

"Papa," I asked, "any word from her?"

"From who," Mama interrupted, "the thief?"

"Please . . ." I wanted to tell Mama she shouldn't talk about her that way, but how could I when deep down I knew she was right?

"No, my son," Papa said, "nobody has heard anything. Gonzalo is very upset."

Not as much as me, even though he is the father. He didn't leave everything and risk his hide to follow her.

"Where are you going to live?"

I didn't expect that question, that's why I hadn't prepared a response, but I answered so confidently that I surprised myself and I even half believed it.

"With some friends from work. At least until she turns up."

"Don't wait standing up, Marlon. That one has flown the coop," Mama said.

"This is going to be very expensive, *hijo*," said Papa. "We'll call you later."

Hanging up was like dying a little. Some piece of me is always left behind when I say good-bye. I don't know if everybody is slowly killed by good-byes like I am. My hand was still on the receiver, as if I could hold on to the voice for a minute longer, when I heard another voice, Patricia's, closer and colder, saying:

"Wipe that shadow off your face."

I thought she was referring to my sagging spirits, not the several days of hair growth on my cheeks and chin. I wasn't too aware of my appearance, and I thought it was enough that I showered every day.

"There's a razor among the things I brought you," Patricia said. "If you're going to be responsible for cleanliness, it should start with you."

Among the "things" she brought me, I found a nail clipper, cotton balls, and even some aftershave lotion. As if a good odor could get rid of a bad one, I thought as I put a couple of drops on my neck with my finger.

Perfumed and clean-shaven, I went out to confront the first excrements of the day.

Du yu espeek espanich?" asks a man who has sat down in the seat where Charlotte was sitting.

I say *sí*. He smiles happily and wipes the sweat off his forehead with the back of his hand. Then we start in on national origins: he is Salvadoran and he arrived in the United States one month ago.

"Where did you enter?" he asked me. "From above or below?"

Even after so much time here, I guess I still look like an illegal. From below, I answer, and he adds: Now lots of people are entering from above.

"Where are we?" he asks, and looks out the window, even though it's dark outside.

"I'm not sure if we just passed Fayetteville or we're passing it now."

"Is it true they bring dogs on the buses?"

"That's what they say," I tell him.

Again he wipes his sweaty face with his hand.

"Have you traveled a lot by bus?" he asks me.

"Only twice on long trips."

"Have you seen the dogs?"

"No," I tell him. "Not yet, no."

My neighbor takes a deep breath and tosses back the pitch-black lock of hair that was falling over his forehead. His nose is shining in the darkness.

"My name is Gerardo."

"Oh," I answer, and I look outside. In the glass I can see Gerardo's reflection, looking at me.

"And you?" he asks me.

"Me?"

He nods his head.

"Mar . . . Mario," I tell him.

Gerardo holds out his hand to seal our introductions. It is sweaty, like the rest of his body. As soon as he lets go, I wipe off my hand on the seat.

Everyone on this bus wants to sleep. They begin by trying to find a comfortable position on these uncomfortable seats; then they take sleeping pills and pull out the blankets, face masks, and earplugs. While all of them carry out their sleep-seeking rituals, I will continue to be awake, watching for the signs that tell which cities we are passing, the distances we are traveling, and how much longer we have left to go.

"Where are we?" the Salvadoran asks again. He looks like he has been standing under a sprinkler: even his jacket is dripping with sweat. He shows me a torn-up map of the United States. I look for where we're traveling and point to it: Here.

"That's all?" Gerardo asks, disappointed.

I think: It's not so much, just a few hours, fifteen or twenty, much less than a day or a year.

"Are you going to sleep?" he asks me as he struggles with a button, trying to make his seat back recline more than two inches.

"No," I tell him, "I don't think I'll be able to sleep."

"Me neither," he says, probably thinking about the dogs.

There are others who do sleep, lulled by the motor, or because they are blessed with the ability to fall asleep easily, or because they don't have a Reina to meet. I'm tired, too, not from today but from a long time ago. Maybe I'll sleep again once I see her, like I used to sleep when I lived at home, when Reina was just my neighborhood girlfriend, and the problems were more reasonable, and the only thing that finally woke me up was exhaustion from having slept too much, or Mama's voice offering me a cup of coffee, or Papa's cough, which was his way of saying "I'm here." Maybe I'll sleep again when I can sleep next to Reina.

"I've heard that the police set up roadblocks and make everybody get off the bus," Gerardo says to me almost in a whisper.

"That's what they say."

"And that they look through your luggage."

"Yeah, that's what they say."

Gerardo runs his fingers through his slimy hair. It's shining, as if he'd greased it. He turns the light on again and opens up the map.

"Here?" he asks, placing his finger on Fayetteville.

"More or less," I tell him.

Gerardo turns the light off, leans back, and sighs; his eyes, shining and heavy like a manatee's, finally close. The others sleep or pretend to sleep. I envy people who can fall asleep easily, those who when they wake up don't feel like I do, like the weight of their whole life is pressing down on their right foot. That's the foot I wake up on; the one I use to take the first step of the day, to make sure things turn out the way I want them to; the one I step into work with; the one I place first on the airplane to guarantee I have a safe trip; the one I stepped onto this bus with; my right foot, where I put all my hopes and the one I keep my balance on even though I'm sure that the whole thing is a pretty questionable superstition.

One Sunday morning, very early, Reina called me to tell me that the group was ready. What group? I asked her, and she explained that it was our group of traveling companions. "Traveling companions," I thought, as if we were all old friends!

"Did they call you?" I asked.

"Fabiola did," Reina said. "She just called."

"But today is Sunday," I told her, as if the day made any difference.

Fabiola's pressure was working: Reina was worried, upset. They're going to go, she told me, and we still don't have the money.

"That's just that old bi— lady's way of putting pressure on you," I told her.

"Meetings start next week."

Maybe the day of the week did make a difference, because it was Sunday and it felt like I wasn't understanding anything.

"There are some things you can bring and some you can't."

"Like what?" I asked.

"How should I know?" she answered, a little bewildered. "That's what the meetings are for."

At that point, we only had half of what we needed: Reina's desire and her spirit. I wasn't contributing either money or courage, not even desire, which was the least we needed to even get started.

"And the money, Marlon?" Reina asked me.

"Good question."

"This is serious," she said.

"I know," I said, "but where are we going to get it?"

A few days later I learned how true it is when they say that you have to be careful about what you wish for because you might really get it. What that saying doesn't say is to what lengths you should or shouldn't go to get it. In other words, the money came to Reina. It didn't fall from the sky, but she did find it in a drawer.

Aunt Marlén found a mail-order boyfriend through a matchmaker agency. She had already started making excuses, like all the old maids in Colombia, saying things like "Better to dress saints than undress drunkards," when her German man, Halver, appeared. Halver was in his sixties and didn't look at all like a typical German: he was small and had black hair. The only thing Aunt Marlén cared about, though, was that he was a man and that he could walk. At fifty-something, she was going to be a bride. Halver had come from Germany to meet his fiancée, and they were going to get married two weeks later. We had all been involved in their courtship, which had gone on for several months by correspondence. Halver didn't speak Spanish, and Auntie didn't speak German. They decided to write to each other in English, but since neither of them spoke that, the letters sounded like they had been written by Tarzan, and everybody had to help Auntie decode them with a dictionary. Every letter that arrived caused a major to-do, but Aunt Marlén couldn't have been happier. Finally, the long-awaited day arrived when Halver would come to take her back with him to his country.

Like a good fiancé, he came bearing gifts, and like a good, naive tourist, he came loaded with dollars.

"There's something you've got to see," Reina told me, trying to control her emotions.

The good-bye party for the couple was held at our house. Halver was staying with us until their wedding day because Aunt Marlén didn't want to ruin her reputation: it simply wouldn't look right for Halver to live with her before they got married. We'd already had a few shots of rum when Reina took me by the hand and led me into the room where Halver was staying. I thought Reina wanted to mess around a little.

"I locked the door," she told me.

"It'd be better in my room," I suggested as I pulled her toward me. She pushed me away and said: Look what's here. She opened the second drawer of the bedside table. Inside the drawer, all by itself, was an envelope, and dollars were spilling out of it. I practically leaped back and almost smashed into the door.

"You've been looking for this, Reina," I said accusingly.

"No, I haven't," she said. "I found it by accident."

"Nobody opens a drawer by accident," I told her.

"Come here, let's take a look," Reina insisted.

She sat down on the bed looking very satisfied with herself and took the envelope out of the drawer. She told me to keep a lookout while she counted the money. I wanted to shout at her not to do it, to leave it alone; and I could have, because the music was blasting and everybody was laughing loudly trying to understand Halver and him trying to understand them.

"Leave it, Reina, someone might come," I cried under my breath.

"Don't talk to me. I'm counting," she said, and kept counting.

I finished off the rum in the glass I'd carried in there, thinking that Reina's mysterious air was taking a very strange turn. I pressed my ear against the door so I could hear if someone was coming.

"What are you doing, Reina?" I insisted, but she raised her

hand to let me know I shouldn't interrupt her, and she kept counting every single bill in silence.

"Marlon," she said finally, "there's more here than we need."

I tried to get one last drop of rum out of the glass, but all that was left was ice. Reina looked at me without blinking, like she was waiting for something to happen; I looked back at Reina like she had already done what she was thinking of doing.

"No, Reina," I said.

She didn't say anything. She stood up and lifted up her dress; my eyes dropped down to the magnificence of her panties, and I took one step forward, drawn in by false hope. She lowered them a little, letting my eyes feast on that small, well-defined, beautifully tended patch that was destined to make me an accomplice to her crime.

If anyone else had seen what I saw, they would have said I was in the right; they also would have been in a daze and kept their mouths shut, like I did, especially when I saw her stroking those sweet hairs right before she stuffed in the wad of bills; she saw me drooling while I watched her pull up her underpants, pull down her dress, and to top it off, smile as she patted the bundle she was now carrying between her legs. The smile vanished when we heard a knock on the door. Reina quickly put the empty envelope back into the drawer and pushed it closed. I was totally paralyzed, so she had to open the door. It was Aunt Marlén.

"It locked by itself," said Reina, as cool as can be.

"I'm looking for Halver's camera," my aunt said, glowing. "He wants to take pictures of everybody."

Aunt Marlén walked straight over to the bedside table. This was the first time since I had started going along with Reina's idea that I felt like I was dying, especially when I was hoping for Reina to rescue me with a reassuring look in her eyes and I saw that she was gone. Aunt Marlén turned on the lamp and opened the drawer.

"Here it is," she said happily.

On the way out, she pinched my cheek tenderly and whispered in my ear:

"You're all sweaty, you little devil."

I walked out of the room and down the hall, leaning against the wall for support. I reached the room where everybody was gathered and saw that Reina was dancing with Juancho Tirado. She winked at me when she saw me. Aunt Marlén tried without much luck to get all of us into a group for a picture. Papa came up to me looking concerned:

"What's going on?"

"Nothing."

"Had too much rum?"

"Yeah, must be that."

"Gotta take it easy, *hijo*."

If only that had been the problem, I thought, that I had been drinking too much, like Papa thought. I wish I'd had a head on my shoulders to think about the consequences, but that night I was in some kind of stupor watching Reina, happy and sassy, dancing shamelessly with those thousands of dollars stuffed into her pussy.

"You didn't have any money left?" Patricia asked me.

If Reina had known where all those dollars were going to end up, she'd have rather they'd rotted right there in her underpants.

"No," I said.

"And she didn't, either?"

"Reina? Why do you ask? What has she got to do with it?"

Both our minds were wandering during this conversation. Patricia was thinking about me and finding me a place to live; I was remembering Reina so full of herself with all that money between her legs.

"If she wants to look for you, she's also going to need money," Patricia said, "just like you."

"Neither of us had a penny left," I repeated.

"I'll be right back," Patricia said, and walked away.

I was tired. I'd been tired since I arrived, but today I'd been through the ordeal of the first day on the job, and I was ready to get out of there. It was late, and I still didn't know where I was going to stay or what time it was.

"What time is it?" I asked somebody on his way out of the kitchen.

"Time to go home," he said in English.

"Gracias," I said to him, but I wasn't any the wiser for his answer. I figured it must be pretty late by looking at everybody's tired faces.

Patricia returned, dressed to go out. I was still thinking about what she had said to me and I asked her:

"Patricia, how do you go about finding somebody who's lost?"

"That depends, *mijo*."

"On what?"

"On lots of things," she said, "but mostly on how much money you have."

Which meant we were screwed. If it was a question of money, we'd never find each other.

"It's like everything else in life," Patricia told me. "In any case, the way to start is by looking."

"Where do I start looking?"

"By looking for a place to live," she said, and then smiled. "I've got something for you, temporary and not so great, but they'll let you stay a few nights."

"And then?"

"Then we'll see. Let's go outside; somebody's coming by to pick you up."

On the way out Patricia explained to me what was going on. She had called, she told me, a very good man: "better than bread," were her exact words. He would pick me up and take me to a place where I could sleep, take a shower, and have breakfast. Did you bring your things? Patricia asked me, because you'll need them there, she said. And where is there? I thought to ask.

"It's just for a few nights," she said without really answering my question, "and after that we'll find something better."

That "something better" kept echoing in my head, like a question that hadn't been answered. I thought I really should follow up on it. Patricia looked at me, but when she started talking, the train passed over our heads, and the racket drowned out our voices as it shook the whole street and the metal structure. When it was silent again, I felt kind of uncomfortable insisting on it. It seemed wiser to change the subject and ask her about the man who was picking me up. Who is this guy, Patricia?

"He is a saint, kind of like the pope of Queens."

"What's his name?" I asked, as if a name could tell you something about a person. Or maybe it could.

"Orlando, his name is Orlando," she said, and looked up at the sky as if Orlando had already achieved his deserved reward.

"Where's he from?" I asked, because our nationality does say something about who we are.

"Ah, *mijo*," Patricia said, her gaze still lost in the distance, "this man is not from here, from this earth; he must be from the beyond, from another planet, wherever angels come from."

We were already waiting outside when we saw the angel drive up in a black Mercedes-Benz, a pretty old model, but anyway a Mercedes. The man put his hand out the window and waved to Patricia and she said, in a state of ecstasy:

"That's him, *mijo*. Go quickly."

I was going to get into a car with a stranger who was going to take me somewhere, and the only thing I knew about it was that there were other places that were better. Okay, I thought, there's always somewhere better, and anyway, I kept thinking, what could I lose when the lost person was me? I mumbled:

"Patricia . . ."

"Get going, *mijo*, don't make him wait. I'll expect you tomorrow at ten o'clock."

I said a quick good-bye and hurried to the car; the people waiting in cars behind him began to shout and honk. Orlando told me to hurry.

"These people don't know what patience is," he said, a little rattled as I sat down. "You can tell they've never had to wait. Oh, I'm so sorry: I'm Orlando." And he held his hand out to me.

Orlando, the angel, must've weighed about two hundred pounds: much bigger and heavier than any angel should be if he wants to fly, and the rolls of flesh didn't leave any room between his belly and the steering wheel. Orlando was huge, and like all Colombians, he had a mustache.

"Patricia told me that your girlfriend is lost," Orlando said. I hadn't thought of it in those terms: I always thought that I was the one who was lost.

"We both got lost," I said, then explained, "We lost each other."

"Just a second," he told me, "because now I don't know where I am."

He stopped the Mercedes and looked toward the corner. "I haven't been here for a while," he explained.

"Okay, carry on," he said once he had oriented himself and taken off. I didn't feel like telling my story, but since he was helping me, I had to go over it again. I still hadn't totally dismissed the possibility that by telling it again and again, I'd finally see the light that would lead me back to her.

"You don't remember anything?" Orlando asked me when I'd finished.

"There was a sign in front of the building," I told him, "with big letters that said 'Queen.'"

"Queen or Queens?"

I didn't know that one letter could have so much meaning, that my return might depend on it.

"Queen. That's my girlfriend's name."

"Queen?" Orlando asked.

"Reina," I said in a defeated tone of voice, the way we say the names of the people who are no longer with us.

We sat in silence for a few minutes. Orlando was driving the Mercedes as if it was an old horse that knew its own way, and I looked dejectedly at the landscape full of houses, telephone poles, gas stations, places that sell food, so much food it wasn't hard to understand why Orlando was as big as he was.

"Where are we going?" I asked, breaking the silence.

"Didn't Patricia tell you?"

"Yes," I answered, "but while she was telling me, a train passed right over our heads and I couldn't hear anything."

"That one stops right near where we're going," he told me. "You can take it tomorrow and it will leave you at the door of your work."

"And what if I get lost?"

Orlando wanted to laugh. I could see that he was making an effort to control himself; it's understandable, nobody these days would think that somebody could get lost and never return.

"Relax," he said. "I'll send one of the alcoholics with you to the station."

I laughed because I thought it was a joke that I didn't understand and that it was only polite to laugh, but Orlando was still serious; then I realized that it wasn't a joke, but I still didn't understand.

"They could even accompany you all the way to work," he continued. "Some are already working, they're well on their way to recovery. You'll know who I'm talking about at the meeting."

What? I blamed it on my tiredness. I thought that maybe those few days when I hadn't been me had caused some kind of brain damage, or maybe it was impossible for people to understand each other in New York.

"Where are we going, Orlando?"

"To the alcoholics," he said. "Where else? We're almost there."

I wanted to tell him that I wasn't an alcoholic, ask him where he was taking me, tell him to let me off right there. But what could I do, go back to the middle of nowhere? A freeway and nowhere are the same thing, and a labyrinth and this city, and a fat angel and a devil could also be confused. Anyway, angels don't have mustaches, and there is no heaven in New York.

"Where are we going, Orlando?"

Take me anywhere, do anything with me, just don't send me back, out of New York. She must be here, I can feel her footsteps; it smells like Reina and like booze. Where are we going, Orlando?

"To the drunkards. We're almost there."

"Speak! Speak! Speak!" they shouted in chorus as they slapped me on the back. "Speak! Speak! Speak!"

I felt just like I used to on school field trips, when the kids in the back would taunt the ones in the front by singing: "The donkeys in the front go la-la-la . . ." Even though it was far away, New York was not a field trip and the people shouting here were alcoholics. They had woken me up at seven in the morning, and I had barely slept because of all the excitement.

"Are you the newcomer?" is what I woke up to as somebody pulled on my foot. I was so afraid I couldn't even answer. "They told me to get the newcomer," the alcoholic who woke me up insisted.

I asked where Orlando was, then remembered that he had dropped me off and left, saying: I'll be back tomorrow, but you'll be in good hands here; then he'd turned to a woman and said: Margarita, I'm leaving this kid with you, take good care of him; and Margarita came up to me, looking at me the way you might look at a slab of meat, and said: The kid's not bad. Orlando pulled me away from her and said to me: She used to work the streets, but here she's recovering. Then he added: Don't pay any attention if you see them fighting. Nothing really bad ever happens. The house was horrible, huge and falling apart; it smelled like soup and air freshener, and even though it was late, men and women were wandering around everywhere like drunken ghosts.

"The meeting starts at seven-thirty," said the man who woke me up. "Go take a shower, newcomer."

The men slept on one floor and the women on another, and there were four or five beds in each room. One bathroom upstairs, another downstairs, a kitchen, a recreation and meeting room, and posters everywhere on the walls that said LIVE AND LET LIVE; FIRST THINGS FIRST; THINK, THINK, THINK; GRANT ME THE SERENITY TO ACCEPT THE THINGS I CANNOT CHANGE, and other things like that.

"I don't have to go to the meeting," I protested, but he grabbed my foot again, probably thinking I had been drinking, and insisted:

"Everyone here has to go, it's one of the rules," and he began to recite them to me one by one. But when he said, "You don't get breakfast if you don't go to the meeting," I obeyed right away.

At the meeting they served coffee. Everybody had to attend, and there I was among this strange assortment of creatures: a bunch of drunks, whores, and drug addicts, all of them as poor as rats.

"Speak! Speak!"

They all stared at me as they chanted, insisting I go up to the front and tell my story: The newcomer is going to tell us about his struggle with drugs and alcohol. Let's welcome our *compañero* who has decided to give himself another chance; all of this spoken in Colombian, Puerto Rican, Central American accents, and even though they insisted they were sober, they still sounded like drunks.

"There's some kind of mistake," I told them. "I'm here for a different reason."

"Speak! Speak!"

Margarita took my hand and pulled on it until I stood up, then led me up to the stage, placed me behind the lectern, and said euphorically:

"A round of applause for our new *compañero*!"

All I could do was smile, and then I began to introduce myself like an alcoholic from Ecuador had done, even though he never finished his speech because he forgot what he was saying right in the middle.

"Good morning." I was going to say *"compañeros,"* but my self-respect wouldn't let me. "Good morning, my name is Marlon Cruz," and I was going to continue, but they started applauding. I said I was Colombian, and they applauded; I told them how old I was, and they continued to applaud. I told them I was lost, but not in drugs or alcohol, really actually lost, and they clapped even louder. I told them I was looking for my girlfriend, they applauded; that her name was Reina and she had different-colored eyes, in other words, one of her eyes was lighter than the other, and that if anybody knew anything about her would they please tell me, and they burst into a round of applause, and I said to myself: Jesus, this is great, I've never gotten so much applause in my life.

Later, around eight o'clock, they finally gave me breakfast, accompanied me to the subway, and I arrived at work at ten.

"That place is horrible."

"I know, *hermano*, I've been there," Giovanny said, "but it's just until something else works out."

"But Giovanny, it's for drunks and whores, faggots and crazies." Then I said, "I could go crazy there."

And that was as far as the conversation got because Don Pastor arrived with his not-very-friendly face.

"Good morning, Don Pastor," we both greeted him.

"Good morning, Giovanny."

Don Pastor went into the kitchen and Giovanny followed him. I went to the bathrooms and found that they had already been pissed in. At that moment I wanted the toilets to swallow me up. I wondered what I was doing in this country full of pissers.

Then Patricia arrived to take a piss.

"Good morning, *mijo*, how did it go?"

"Bad, Patricia."

"Why? Didn't you sleep well?"

"No, it's not that. It's just that, Patricia, that place really isn't for me."

"I know, *mijo*, but I doubt you'll be able to find anything better for free."

Patricia looked in my eyes and saw the problem and said:

"Let's see what I can drum up."

But it wasn't Patricia who got me out of that house; it was Margarita. The following night I arrived so late and so tired that I couldn't even think about where I was, and I fell right to sleep. A while later, I don't know how long, I heard a voice next to my ear whispering: Hey, do me a favor and eat me out. I thought I was dreaming—who wouldn't have thought so?—then I felt a toothless mouth nibbling on my ear and I screamed.

"Eat me out, please, eat me out," Margarita begged, lying down next to me, her tits in the air, rubbing her big stinking cunt.

I screamed again and someone turned on the light. Three alcoholics had woken up and one was still sleeping. Margarita was begging and crying and one of them insulted her:

"Whore, fatso, get out of here, you *conchatumadre*!"

The other two were more excited and egged her on.

"You eat him, Margarita, eat him up!"

I leaped out of bed, rushed into the bathroom, and locked myself in; bathrooms had started to be an important part of my personal space, my putrid bubble. I sat down on the floor, swearing and shivering. I swore that I would leave that house that very night, that I'd rather sleep in the street than stay here another night.

I waited until I didn't hear any shouting, then went to get my stuff, opening the door very quietly so nobody would hear me. I felt so strange, like somebody stealing something that belongs to him. As I got closer to the room, I realized that Margarita was still in there; I thought I heard her crying very softly, almost to herself. The light was off, but the door was open. I crept in slowly, trying to see where Margarita was. If she was still in my bed, I would have to wait to get my stuff. By the light from the street, I could see that my bed was empty, that all the residents were out of their beds, and that Margarita wasn't crying: she was moaning. She was lying on the floor, completely naked, and the drunks were standing in line above her. One by one they were going down on Margarita.

I never went back there. Later I found out from Orlando that the house had been demolished. The monster, forever growing, was extending its tentacles beyond Manhattan, knocking down all the old buildings and replacing them with new ones.

When Orlando arrived the next morning and opened the front door, he tripped over my legs; I'd fallen asleep on the floor, hugging the bag that carried all the things Patricia had given me.

"What do we have here?" Orlando asked.

"It's me," I mumbled, stiff and half asleep. I told him what had happened and begged him not to bring me back here, to help me find somewhere else to go, anywhere, but that I couldn't come back to that house.

"I can't do it, Orlando, I just can't," I told him. He had a worried look on his face, and he seemed to be talking to himself when he mumbled his words:

"That's the trouble with whores. They can't seem to find any other way of dealing with their problems."

He drove me to the restaurant.

When I started seriously looking for Reina, I went many times to see Orlando at his office. Anybody who had a problem went to him: the bankrupt, the needy, the sick, the unemployed, the confused, and even the bored. In other words, everybody.

I went to find out if he knew anything about what I was looking for, or if he knew of anyone who was looking for me. But he didn't know anything about either the one or the other.

"Give me all the information and we'll see what happens."

Nothing happened, not through him, anyway, even though Orlando did ask everybody who came to his office about her.

"She's got different-colored eyes, so it's easy to identify her."

It was as if Reina wasn't letting anybody see her face, as if she was wearing sunglasses, or had gone up in smoke. Nobody even knew about anybody who looked like her at all.

My eyes are closing and my mouth is floating open. I am struggling against time and exhaustion, against the drone of the tired engine and the monotonous landscape, which are both lulling me with: Sleep, Marlon, we're not going to get there any sooner if you stay awake. I'm going to call her first thing in the morning. I'm so close it would probably be a better idea to tell her that I'll be there that night, better because then we'll both know what's in store for us. I've got a lot to do at the first place we stop in the morning: eat breakfast, change clothes, shave, call Reina. All in the fifteen minutes this jerk always gives us.

"In a few minutes we'll be arriving in Manning," the driver says over the loudspeakers, then adds sarcastically, "but you never know, because there are federal agents just swarming the place, looking for illegals hiding in Greyhound buses, but Greyhound ain't no hideout for *bandidos*."

Nobody dares say a word. We know he's the kind of guy who really is capable of ordering the bus to be searched, the typical Yankee hunter kind of guy, the one who's a cop to the core, even if he doesn't wear a uniform. Gerardo looks at me with his mouth hanging open and tells me, stammering, that he's going to the bathroom. With the concern of a true professional, I warn him:

"That bathroom is very dirty; maybe you should wait until we stop."

But Gerardo is already running to the back of the bus. All I care about is that we keep going south, burning up the pavement until the last driver says: Welcome to Miami, welcome, Marlon, to your kingdom, to your reigning queen. This is the last place your cowardly and frightened feet will take you, where your exhaustion will come to an end; now you can open your eyes, wake up, we're there.

"Wake up, everybody. We are about to arrive in Manning."

Welcome, stranger."

Giovanny, who I had begun to think of as my only friend, was still standing behind me. We were both scanning the room. Or maybe we just wanted to confirm what they had said about the building, explain the faces they all pulled when they found out I was going to live on Northern Boulevard, in the building on the corner of Northern Boulevard.

"Holy shit!" one of the guys at the restaurant said in English, and others said other things.

"Do you like racquetball?" somebody else asked, and the others started laughing.

"What's going on, Giovanny?" I asked.

"Don't pay any attention to them," he told me. "If you consider what they're charging you, it'll be fine, you'll get used to it."

Patricia told me: I found you a different place to live. She sounded happy when she said it, so I figured I had nothing to be afraid of. They'll charge you, but not very much, and it's nearby. Giovanny came with me after work, made sure I knew which subway station to get on and which to get off at, talked to me the whole way there, giving me advice about surviving in New York City and other words of encouragement. As we approached, he pointed to the building and I got excited because it looked so new and big and modern.

"That one?" I asked.

"No," he corrected me, "the one next to it."

The one that was old and dirty and small. The two were stuck right up against each other.

"The new one is a sports club for the rich," he said, "and the other one is a rooming house for the poor."

It seemed strange to me that they were so close to each other, it just didn't seem normal; I knew something was up and then Giovanny explained it to me.

"The rich people want to buy, but the poor people don't want to sell. The rich are offering a little and the poor are asking for a lot. The rich and the poor still haven't come to an agreement."

That sounded familiar. Here finally was something I could understand, something that was the same as in Colombia. So in we went to the poor people's building. They'd already told us where we were supposed to go, and since the elevator was out of order, we walked up the stairs to the eighth floor. I looked around suspiciously. It was hard work climbing the stairs, or maybe my legs just didn't want to obey me.

"*Arriba*, brother, we're almost at the top," Giovanny said to lift my spirits.

"This building reminds me of the other one," I told him.

"Which other one? The one I took you to?"

"The first one," I said, "where I went with Reina."

Giovanny stopped and in the darkness I saw the fluorescent whites of his eyes; I could also hear that he was out of breath, just like me.

"Could it be the same one?" Giovanny asked.

"No," I said firmly. "No, it's not."

"Are you sure?" he asked again. "Remember, you weren't you."

"When I ran out I was," I said, then added, "and this isn't the same building."

"Let's keep going." Again I heard his footsteps climbing the stairs.

There was different music playing on every floor; on some, several different kinds at once, and we heard other noises as we climbed. But as we got to the upper stories and the farther up we climbed, the more one particular sound prevailed.

"What's that noise?" I asked Giovanny.

"Balls," he answered.

On the eighth floor we stopped to catch our breath. We had arrived. We turned the light on in the hallway and bumped into an old guy walking around in the dark with his hands deep in the pockets of his bathrobe. His eyes were closed and sunken inside black circles. Giovanny said hi to him, but the old guy didn't answer. Then we looked for the door to room 802. The bell didn't work; before we could knock, it opened.

"Welcome, stranger."

Patricia had probably told him I was coming, but I doubt if she described me to him. Maybe she told him I was lost and he could see the disorientation in my face. The man who opened the door was named Roger Pena, and he was the one we were supposed to see. One of the three beds in his room was unoccupied, and that's what I was going to pay for.

"I will show you around the land of Ithaca so as to convince you," he told me, and Giovanny and I looked at each other, confused. "The bathroom is outside, like all bathrooms are: down the hall and to your right. The kitchen is on your left."

Giovanny was still behind me. I was sure his big eyes were seeing more than mine. That's why I asked him:

"What do you think?"

"Do you have a choice?" Giovanny answered.

The room was small and had only one window. The walls were bare; the room's only decoration was two naked bulbs, facing each other, and so weak that I didn't think they'd survive getting turned on or off. The floor was covered with a worn-out rug, faded and full of cigarette burns. There was a wardrobe with a cloudy mirror on its door and a bookcase overflowing with books. The room smelled like food, and one of the beds was bigger than the other two.

"The big one is mine," Roger Pena said, then he pointed to one of the small ones and added, "and that one is yours."

It looked a lot like the room Reina and I had ended up in: one window, almost no light, musty and smelling like poverty, the air inside sad and heavy. I already figured she wasn't there anymore, that she was probably with Gloria, her cousin, or whoever it was who talked her into it; Gloria, the one who changed our lives.

"It's really late," Giovanny said. "I've got to go."

I felt like Giovanny was abandoning me forever. I wanted to give him the same kind of hug I'd given my friends when I left. We were speechless and all we had were our hugs to say good-bye with. If any one of us had tried to talk, we would have started crying, and we'd been taught to believe that men don't cry, that a man can't cry for another man, that he can't tell another man that he loves him and is going to miss him. Today more than ever, I really regret that I didn't plant a good-bye kiss firmly on the cheeks of each of my friends.

"See you tomorrow, Giovanny," I said to him in a hollow voice.

"See you tomorrow, brother," he said, and winked his eye, which was so big it didn't quite close all the way.

There I was, alone and with a stranger, feeling like throwing myself facedown on my bed and calling out to my friends to come rescue me. I felt as lonely as I had when I was on the street and just like any other stray dog.

"You can put your things under the bed," Roger Pena told me. "The wardrobe is also mine."

"And the other bed?" I asked.

"You'll never see him. He works while we sleep. Just in case, his name is Javier."

I sat on the bed to check out the mattress. I couldn't feel it, so I picked up the flimsy blanket to see if there even was one. Yeah, it was there, but it was right on the verge of doing a disappearing act.

"Here, kid," Roger Pena said, handing me some keys. "They're yours. Don't lose them, because I'll have to charge you for duplicates. One is to the door of the building and the other to the room. If you go out without locking the door, I can guarantee that you won't find even the floor when you get back, and you'll owe me for everything as if it was new."

In spite of the lightbulbs, I didn't manage to see what this man looked like. He spoke slowly and confidently, and he walked around the room as if it was a grand salon. He wore a bathrobe like millionaires wear in the movies and slippers and socks that somehow didn't seem appropriate for his age, though I wasn't really able to figure out how old he was.

"You always pay for the week in advance," he continued. "But Patricia asked me to let you slide for the first week. It's Patricia I'm doing the favor for."

Sometimes it happened that I felt the entire weight of New York City—its millions of inhabitants; its blocks of cement, iron, and glass; its tons of garbage; its time and energy; the river of shit in its drainpipes; the madness and the blood—all pressing down on me like an iron in God's hand.

"The light gets turned off at twelve," Roger Pena said in a heavy voice. "If it's dark when you arrive, don't even think of turning it on. How long you plan on staying?"

"Not long," I told him. "I'm looking for my girlfriend. When she turns up, I'll be leaving with her."

"Where is she?"

"I don't know. I'm looking for her."

"In New York."

"Yeah."

That was the first time I heard Roger Pena's laugh, a rusty laugh that had nothing to do with joy or a sense of humor. I would hear it very rarely afterward, and then mostly to express sarcasm rather than in reaction to something funny or happy.

I don't know if it was the time of day or the room, but I felt terrible. I wanted to open the window, but I'd already found out that even though I was paying, the only thing I had a right to do in that room was go to sleep. I was feeling so bad, in fact, that everything started to move.

"That bag is moving," I told Roger Pena, starting to feel even dizzier. He went over to the corner and carefully lifted the small suitcase that was moving on its own. He opened the zipper and a little dog stuck its head out. Roger Pena stroked it and talked to it like it was a baby. It wasn't as if the dog was horrible or anything, but I felt nauseated.

"What's that?" I asked, pointing to the animal.

"What does it look like to you?" Roger Pena asked, showing him to me.

"What's his name?"

"Demon."

"Demon? What does it mean?"

"Devil."

"Why did you name him that?"

"Because he's a son of a bitch."

He opened the zipper all the way, took him out, and held him gently in his arms. He cooed to him and looked at him with infinite tenderness.

"Does he bite?" I asked, afraid.

"Of course he bites," Roger said. "When somebody messes with us, he bites."

"What kind of dog is he?"

"A mongrel, like you and me," he said. Then he looked at me and added, "He's a Colombian dog."

He put him back in the bag and reassured him with terms of endearment and promises of treats in the morning. Then he looked at his watch and said:

"It's twelve o'clock."

He pulled down the covers on his bed, and before I could even ask him to wait a minute so I could put away my things, he turned off the light.

I could just barely make things out in the darkness, and I saw, with the help of the light from outside, that Roger Pena had already gotten into bed. I took off my clothes and left for tomorrow what I wasn't able to do today. I got in between the strange sheets that smelled like somebody else, and in the silence and the dark, I heard that noise again.

"What's that noise?" I asked him, figuring he was still awake.

"A ball," he answered from his corner.

I closed my eyes and tried to imagine what kind of ball it could be and what a ball was doing at that hour of the night bouncing against a wall. I also asked myself what meaning life could possibly have in this room next to this very strange man I had just met, with a dog who slept in a bag, with the threat of another stranger appearing at any moment, and with a ball bouncing off the wall my pillow was leaning against.

As I lay there awake, I thought that until I found Reina, I would live through whatever hell New York had to offer. That I'd better be patient because I probably wouldn't have even one day of relief.

Everyone at home knew that Halver's money had been stolen, and even though they never found any proof, Mama started making insinuating remarks about Reina and how much she'd been drinking that night, the way she was dancing, and how she'd been poking around in the bedrooms.

"Where she had no business going, because she hadn't lost anything," Mama said.

Then came the interrogation session with trick questions that made me break out in a sweat. They wanted to know if it was true that Reina was planning a trip, that Reina loved money, that her father wasn't doing that well in his job, that this and that that; and if I knew anything about the theft, I should come clean, that everybody would forgive me.

"I don't know anything, Mama."

"You didn't use to be like this, Marlon."

"But Mama . . ."

"You didn't use to be like this."

I'd never fallen in love before. They'd never seen me in the clouds, staring off into space, thinking about a woman, or shut up in my room listening to music, imagining my life with her in New York, where she would finally give herself to me, when we would finally do, consummate, what was still left undone.

"Marlén and Halver are not going to be able to go on their cruise in the Caribbean," Mama said loudly, frowning and looking at me like I was a hardened criminal. I didn't say another word. There was nothing left for me to do. I just felt sad when I saw Aunt Marlén crying like a little girl, trying to explain to Halver with her three words of English that we weren't really like that. Halver answered her in German.

"He's barking at me!" my aunt said, about to faint.

"No, Auntie," I comforted her, "that's just how Germans talk."

Aunt Marlén and Halver had to spend their honeymoon at a friend's ranch about two hours outside Medellín.

"They shouldn't complain, at least they'll have good weather," Reina told me, then added with irritation, "Anyway, what's the big deal? Isn't it the same thing to get laid here or in Timbuktu?"

"But didn't you say that it would be different in New York? That that's why we're waiting to do it there?"

"That's different," she said. "We're leaving for good, and your aunt is just going there to lose her virginity."

We laughed quietly, almost guiltily, and felt very naughty, as if we were already in the New York that we had invented for ourselves, the one Reina invented for me so that I'd go with her where she believed she'd find happiness. Reina laughed until her belly ached, and then she asked me:

"Do you have any idea where Timbuktu is?"

I looked at her without smiling; I scanned her coolly and I said to her: It's here, pointing to my crotch where the swelling could be seen through my pants. Reina reached out her hand and grabbed it, the zipper came down slowly, and I closed my eyes; and with my eyes closed I said to her:

"You're going to kill me if you don't give it to me."

"I'll give it to you in New York," she repeated. Then she told me we had to go. I remembered that we were meeting with Fabiola and the others who were planning to travel with us. Reina said matter-of-factly: We're all ready.

Fabiola, perfumed and smiling, greeted us. She even had the nerve to speak to us in English right in the middle of downtown Medellín.

"Guelcom, guelcom." I'm sure that's the only word she knew.

There were faded posters of the Statue of Liberty, San Francisco, Chicago, and Miami hanging on the walls of the dark old office. On a blackboard she had written in big letters: PARADISE TRAVEL: WE COME THROUGH FOR YOU. Ten ridiculous-looking figures were sitting in a circle in silence. Fabiola invited us to sit down and join the group, and I, who hated anything to do with joining in or being forced to socialize, obeyed without protesting. Fabiola spoke, almost in ecstasy:

"We're all here."

Holding her two index fingers straight up and pointing, like she was getting ready to conduct an orchestra, she began her speech, full of smiles and melodious tones: We do come through for you, she said, and we have the necessary contacts to guarantee that all of you will get through into the United States a few days after you leave here. How many? Nobody knows. Everything depends on the circumstances. This is the first of three meetings, and these three meetings will turn us into a kind of family, because as soon as we reach Guatemala, we will have to pretend to be a group of friends on vacation, do you understand? Yes, *señora*, the fools answered in unison, and among the voices I heard was Reina's: she listened with full attention to every single word Fabiola said.

One by one I looked at the members of my new family: a bunch of pathetic individuals they wouldn't even let into hell. They carried in their expressions all the despair and fatigue of having used up every possible option in this country. This country, *este país*, we all call it, with a tone of disrespect that is always accompanied by a look of disgust. As if *este país* was some dirty rag, somebody else's, not something every one of us had created.

"Are you paying attention?" Reina whispered to me.

Fabiola continued with her list of instructions: After the next meeting she will need to receive money from everybody who is planning to make the trip; we shouldn't tell anybody about it; we should get rid of every piece of paper that has any reference to Paradise Travel written on it; again, welcome, and she congratulated us for having chosen them and trusted them to fulfill our biggest and most glorious dream.

"Guelcom, guelcom," she repeated with another big smile, and Reina sat up tall and happy. "Does anybody have any questions?"

Everybody looked at each other, feeling awkward about not having any questions to satisfy Fabiola. They were all clearing their throats except one who was staring right at me, a young woman, though older than us, who was wearing a skirt so short that when she uncrossed her legs I could see that she wasn't wearing anything underneath. My eye itched and she looked at me like she was feeling sorry for me as Reina elbowed me.

"What the hell . . . ," Reina blurted out, then she looked at Fabiola and said, "I have a question."

"Yes, dear."

"When are we leaving?"

Fabiola celebrated the question with a wide smile.

"When I get all the money," she said. "Then we can set the dates, but remember: you've only got until next week. At the next meeting we'll talk about what you have to do, what you can bring, and then we'll know who's in and who's out."

Reina left feeling satisfied. Now she had what she didn't have before: dollars and even more than she needed; and she had somebody to accompany her on her adventure. Even so, as happy as she was, she said to me:

"So I wonder who you're going with, that slut or me."

"What slut?" I asked her.

"If you keep acting like an ass, you'll stay here."

They say that whoever's got the money makes the conditions, and in this project, she was in charge of everything. She had the money and the desire, and she didn't need anybody; she could do it all by herself. That's why many times I wondered why Reina needed to take me along. And even though I suspected the answer, it seemed totally inconceivable to me that I had such good luck.

Soon other days would come, everyday kinds of days, days that all seem so much like one another that you can easily forget which day it is. This always happens when you don't expect anything out of time anymore, so you don't even need to count the days. I'd finally gotten over all the turmoil that hope can bring you. When I saw that Reina hadn't appeared for a week, two weeks, for a month, two months, I began to understand that instead of time being on my side, it was against me.

I spent the little money I earned on the most immediate chances of finding her. Almost all of it on calls to Medellín to ask if anybody had heard from her; her father had to know something, she couldn't have just disappeared. The earth doesn't just swallow somebody up, not if she's still alive.

"You know more than Gonzalo," Juancho Tirado told me once when I wasted a phone call on him.

On another call, Eduardo Montoya told me, "Gonzalo can barely talk, but he doesn't know anything."

And Carlitos:

"Gonzalo has aged a lot since Reina left."

Ungrateful Reina, I thought, who doesn't even feel sorry for her own father. Or . . . what could have happened to her that has made it so she couldn't call?

"Maybe they picked her up," Giovanny Fonseca said, and I felt that strange combination of happiness and sadness all at the very same moment. It was painful to imagine Reina in jail, but any chance of finding her always gave me hope.

"How can we find out?" I asked.

"Orlando," Giovanny said, and that day, instead of having lunch, I went to find him.

Orlando was eating. He told me that if I didn't mind, I could talk to him while he ate, because his meals lasted a long time. I told him what I was worried about, and with his mouth full, he answered:

"I'm going to tell you something very serious, my boy. Neither you nor Reina exists in this country. You came in through a black hole and the computers don't know anything about you. This is fine if you don't want them to find you, but bad if you're looking for someone."

He took another huge bite, so big this time that he had to wait before starting to talk again.

"But if she's been arrested, it'll be easier to find her," Orlando continued. "Give me a description of her and a few days."

Two days is a long time when you are waiting anxiously and when it's an effort just to get out of bed in the morning, and a bigger one to clean toilets, and when it even feels like an effort to get a little rest. I had a really hard time sleeping in that room, and when summer began and the nights started getting hotter, I preferred to spend them on that rooftop where Giovanny took me to give me a dose of reality and look out over Manhattan. From there you could feel the breeze from the river, and it was quieter than in that room even though you could hear the hum of the city. I would stay and watch the lights of the monster until the sun began to shed its own light on it. Sometimes I managed to sleep a little, at least a little more than New York, which never slept. Whenever I'd fall asleep, I'd dream about her: Reina hugging the Empire State Building like King Kong, lifting the torch on top of the Statue of Liberty, as a top model in a lighted billboard over Times Square, like a mermaid run aground along the banks of the Hudson, or clicking her high-heeled shoes down Forty-second Street. All this time, that's the only place I've seen her: in my dreams and my nightmares.

"She hasn't been arrested," Orlando told me two days later, and then added without any bad intention, "Maybe you should look for her in the morgue."

This didn't upset me because I didn't even consider it a possibility.

"No, Don Orlando. I'm sorry to contradict you, but don't bother looking for Reina among the dead, because she's alive."

He snorted and leaned back, not really objecting to my being disrespectful, but as if he was asking how I could be so sure.

"She's alive," I repeated. "That's the one thing I do know."

I still didn't know that a disappearance is worse than a death, or that it is a different kind of death. Death without the dead.

"We've got to keep looking for her, Don Orlando. Please help me."

"Okay, kiddo," he said, "but don't get your hopes up. This city swallows people up."

Hope fades, you get used to the pace, you start to betray your own dreams, you stop crying, but you also stop laughing, and finally you end up with the immigrant's curse: you don't want to stay, but you don't want to go back, either.

"Why go back?" Roger Pena asked me one night after we'd gotten to know each other a little better. "So they can kill us?"

He said it without anger as he petted Demon, who closed his eyes with each stroke.

I had other reasons not to go back, other than the ones Roger Pena talked about. Most people would say that there can't be any reason stronger than avoiding death, but I'm sure that everybody here has a stronger reason and that's really the reason they stay.

"Maybe you just end up forgetting to go back," I told him.

Roger Pena stood up and walked around the room carrying Demon, then asked in a sarcastic tone of voice:

"Like the lotus-eaters? No, *niño*," he told me, "that was then. Today, men turn into shit-eaters."

He stopped petting Demon and put him back into the bag.

"Why do you keep him closed up inside the bag?" I asked him.

"To train him," he answered, picking him up again and kissing him. Then he closed the zipper. He looked at his watch and said: It's twelve o'clock. Without another word, he stopped talking and turned off the light. He never even said, See you tomorrow.

"Does that noise ever stop?" I asked, even though I knew he wasn't going to answer me.

I got used to the sound of the ball hitting the wall, to the room's squalor, to Javier's nonpresence, to Roger's strange way of talking, and to his farts and snores. I couldn't say that I was getting used to living in New York; I guess I was resigning myself to it, which is different, and like a parasite I was learning to live in the intestines of the beast and feed off it, always careful not to provoke my host.

People got used to me, too, or resigned themselves, like you resign yourself to being around certain relatives you have to put up with because they are part of the family; all that sissy stuff about tolerance and harmony, but if it depended on you, you'd have killed them or never had anything to do with them in the first place. Pastor Gómez got used to me and stopped looking at me like I was some piece of trash that had blown into his restaurant off the street. He had nothing to complain about, anyway, because I wasn't sleeping in his basement anymore, I always arrived on time in the morning, and at night I was never in a rush to leave. If the toilets weren't shining it was because they were too old, but he never found any drops of urine, any pubic hairs, or any smears of shit that I hadn't cleaned up. Sometimes they smelled bad, but then people don't shit roses.

"Pastor is very pleased with your work," Patricia told me.

I thought that his being pleased might mean a raise or a promotion, but it still didn't go beyond praise. Don Pastor was also pleased to be paying me less than he should. Once he called for me and I thought that he could only want me for two things: to fire me or to give me a raise. But it turned out to be neither.

"Did that girl turn up?" he asked me.

I responded a little irritably because of the way he referred to her, not using her name and all: No, *señor*, she hasn't turned up.

"And her family doesn't know anything?"

"She's only got a father and he doesn't know anything. He's very depressed and very ill."

"What kind of a woman is this?" Don Pastor asked angrily.

"Who knows what she's gotten herself into, Don Pastor."

"You've been worse off," he said, "but at least you called home."

"Yes, *señor*," I said softly.

If I was conscious at all of the days passing, it was only because of the calls I was expecting. Papa would tell me: I'll call you next week, on Friday, and then I'd start to count the hours and the days left until then. Or Juancho Tirado would tell me: Call me on Monday to find out if I've heard anything about her; but never were Reina and a Monday further away from each other. Then I realized that I wasn't calling where I should be calling. If there was anybody I should talk to, it was the only other person most affected by this.

"Good evening, Gonzalo, it's me, Marlon."

There was a long silence on the other end. In the background I could hear the sound of the television.

"Gonzalo," I repeated. "Please, I can only talk for five minutes."

"Marlon," he said.

It was like listening to some part of Reina. There's so much of our parents in each of us, so many gestures, obsessions, ways of seeing things, and then there's something in the eyes and the voice.

"There's no news, Marlon," he said, dragging out each syllable.

"It's very strange."

"Not really," Gonzalo said. "She turned out just like Raquel."

You could hear the scars left by years of denial and anger. His silences made me feel that he had already given up.

"I'm going to keep looking for her," I told him.

"Oh," he responded.

And since my wallet wasn't full enough to pay for "ohs," I said good-bye.

"I'll let you know if I hear anything, Gonzalo."

"Marlon!" he said before hanging up. "Maybe it would be easier if you first found Raquel."

If it was difficult to find one person, how would it be to find two? One was a big enough job for me and everybody else. But one thing had become very clear: Medellín was not the place to look for Reina.

"What do I do now?" I asked Giovanny.

"Let's narrow down our possibilities, brother."

Our list began with the prisons.

"Orlando said she wasn't there," I told him.

Then he suggested hospitals and then he apologized and mentioned the morgue.

"She's not there, either," I insisted.

"Anyway," said Giovanny, "without the social, they wouldn't admit her."

"What about the consulate?" I asked.

He told me to remember how we had entered. Since she's undocumented, she wouldn't show up there, either.

"But Orlando can help you. Everyone knows him."

Orlando told me when I visited him: Give me a few days.

"You could also ask about Gloria," I told him.

"What Gloria?"

"Gloria, her cousin."

"Gloria what?" Orlando asked.

Reina had invented a cousin, but this Gloria person did exist, because we both called her, and we both heard her voice on the answering machine. I also saw her in the pictures that she had sent, like a fishing hook, to Reina. But since I had swallowed whole her story about her being a relative, I never asked for a last name.

"No idea, Don Orlando. I don't know her last name."

"That's really great," he said, and let out an awkward laugh. "Do you have any idea how many Glorias there could be in New York?"

"Well, you could ask about only the Colombian Glorias, Don Orlando."

Now he really started to laugh hard. His huge belly rose and fell, and the buttons on his shirt looked like they were about to pop.

"Oh, Marlon," he said, out of breath, "we've got *glorias* even in our national anthem."

But there's not many Reinas, not many queens, even if we had a different one for every day, every parade, and every party. If just one of them had gone to the consulate to say that she was lost, surely that Reina, that Reina in trouble, would be just the one I was looking for.

"Go look for her at the fiestas," Patricia suggested.

"Fiestas?"

"Yes, *mijo*," she explained to me. "Here we celebrate the same holidays as there. Even more so."

That I should go to the parks, parades, soccer matches where Colombians played against Colombians. Us against ourselves, as usual. I went one Sunday to one of them, but I didn't find a soccer match; I found a great big outdoor party where some people were also playing some soccer. There was food frying—*fritangas*—music blasting, women with belly buttons hanging out, and little kids speaking English but looking more like the ones who live on the streets in Colombia and you give a few coins to so they'll watch your car instead of steal it, than any gringo kid I'd ever seen. I went around asking for Reina, went up to everyone asking if they had seen her. She has different-colored eyes. On one Sunday alone I met eighty Glorias and not one of them knew Reina. Don't you have a picture? they asked me over and over. Nobody knew anything, maybe because they hadn't seen her or because they were drunk and didn't even understand what I was getting at. I left as soon as I gave up hope of finding out anything there.

"When people leave their own countries, they turn into caricatures of the ones who stay behind," Roger Pena told me when he saw me arrive frustrated and disgusted.

"I didn't leave for myself," I told him. "I left for her."

"The song of the siren, hey kid? But you shouldn't get involved with those people; it's bad enough to run into them on the street or in the subway, but don't go looking for them."

"But Roger, you're Colombian, too."

"One day I will cease to be so," he assured me.

Roger Pena really did seem like he was from a different world. I had to wait for enough nights to pass and for my eyes to get used to the darkness until I could see him as he really was. In the mornings, when I left, I could only see a bump under the covers, but when I got back at night I always found him exactly the same, wearing one of his silk robes and his slippers, heavily perfumed, almost always in front of his wardrobe mirror checking to see that every hair was in place. Roger Pena had left his hair long on one side of his head and had dyed it, not blond but closer to yellow; and he brushed it over his skull to cover his bald spot. I watched him check to make sure that the grease had made his hair able to withstand sudden gusts of wind, and I felt a certain solidarity with him and all bald men.

"Why are you sick of being Colombian?" I asked him.

"Because we are scoundrels," he said angrily, and I thought there must be another story behind that anger. I never found out what it was, but once he said to me:

"I came here with nothing."

I kept looking at him, hoping he would tell me more, but he was busy watching his dog asleep on his lap. It was almost twelve o'clock, and as soon as he'd look at his watch, he'd jump up like a spring and turn off the light. But he continued:

"The only thing I brought was my name, but I've even lost that."

"That isn't your name?" I asked him.

"First I lost the *ñ*. That letter doesn't exist here."

I wanted to ask him how you could speak without one of the letters of the alphabet, and I wanted to know how they said *coño* in English, but he'd already decided to tell me just five seconds of his story.

"It didn't sound right to me to call myself Rogelio Pena, and since I'd already lost the Peña I didn't see why not also lose the Rogelio as well."

"Roger Pena," I said in amazement.

"It sounds more elegant, don't you think?" he asked, smiling.

"And less Colombian," I added.

Roger let out a hoarse laugh, and seeing him like that gave me the confidence to ask him more questions, about how he made a living, for instance, because I was sure he couldn't support himself with the rent me and the guy who was never there paid him. I also wanted to tell him that Colombians weren't the only scoundrels, that all human beings, without exception, are scoundrels and that is why we are hopelessly lost. But midnight struck for Cinderella, and before I even realized it, the only thing I was hearing in the darkness was the sound of balls bouncing off the wall.

"If we could only find out what the girl looks like," Orlando said. He also told me that no Reina had come through the consulate; and there are about fifty thousand Glorias, he added.

I always thought that by talking about Reina, I was describing her, but enthusiasm isn't all you need to send an image telepathically.

"She's got light brown hair and is about this tall." I put my hand about where I remembered her head reached.

"Ay, *muchacho*," Orlando said, shaking with laughter.

"She's pretty," I said, even if Mama did insist otherwise. Her legs are too skinny, Mama used to say; and to finish her off she'd add jokingly: She's got one faded eye. I protested: The problem, Mama, is that you're looking at her from a different angle.

The next time I called, I told Papa, "Papa, I need a picture of Reina. I've got a few in my drawer."

"I don't think so, *hijo*. Your mother burned them a while back."

"What?!" I couldn't understand what Mama was doing digging around in my drawers. "All of them?" I asked.

"Your mother here is saying that if she still had a picture of her, she'd give it to the police."

Everything I tried to do through them was hopeless. I had only my friends to turn to. I assigned them the task of sending me a picture of Reina.

"There are some in the living room in her house," I told Juancho Tirado. "Try to get one that's pretty recent."

"What if Gonzalo won't give it to me?"

"Don't ask for it," I said. "Just take it."

"But I've got to at least get into his house."

"Go on the pretext of paying him a visit and wait for him to fall asleep in front of the television."

A picture arrived two weeks later: Reina in her last year of high school smiling seductively at the camera, the restless look in her eyes betraying the fact that she already had New York on her mind.

"Look at her." I showed it to Giovanny, Patricia, Don Pastor, everybody I talked to. "This is Reina." I sounded like she was standing right in front of us and I was introducing her, but the truth was it was only a piece of paper, the truth we have to resign ourselves to when all we've got left of a person we love is a picture.

"She's very pretty," Patricia said. Don Pastor looked at her and smiled.

"Her eyes are strange," Giovanny said, opening his own eyes all the way.

"She looks like someone," said one of the cooks.

"Like a niece of mine," said another.

"No," protested a waiter, "like someone on television."

The picture got passed around from one person to another, and it was tough for me, all those hands covered in salsa and oil, the careless way people handle things that aren't theirs, seeing Reina being passed around from hand to hand. I wanted everybody to meet her, but I also wanted them to treat her well.

That night I showed the picture to Roger Pena. He put it under the lightbulb, looked at it for a few seconds, and said:

"She doesn't look Colombian." Then he added, "I don't think you'll find her among them."

He meant us, the pariahs of the world, people who have the same dark-colored eyes and hair, people who aren't much taller than an icebox, the direct descendants of the ape, with wide nostrils and thick lips. Roger Pena said it as if the world was divided into human beings and Colombians.

But it was precisely among them that I had to look for her. Where else? I made a couple of copies of the picture and gave them out to the few people I knew. Giovanny promised to show it to some of the customers of Tierra Colombiana, Patricia and the others among their family and friends, Orlando among the thousands who came to him with their problems, and whenever I heard someone with an accent like mine, I said, Excuse me, and asked: Is it possible you might have seen this woman? They'd look at her suspiciously, like I was with the DEA or something, or like Reina was a dead person and this would somehow implicate them in something, but then they'd sigh with relief when they didn't recognize her, and they'd smile and shake their heads: No, we've never seen her.

I can't count the number of times I showed this picture that had gotten so bent up and faded from being touched by so many hands and traveling so far in my pocket. The more the picture deteriorated, the more my fatigue and hopelessness grew. I heard "No" so many times that I started losing my drive. Noes everywhere, even from her house, where I called every once in a while to find out if there was any news.

"Nothing, Gonzalo?"

"Nothing."

"But it's been so long . . ."

"If Reina doesn't turn up soon, she's not going to find me."

I'd end up trying to lift his spirits, me who had called him hoping to get a boost with some good news. Gonzalo's voice sounded worse than mine, even though sometimes I was just pretending so that both of us would be able to nourish false hopes.

"Sometimes I wonder if she's still alive," he'd say.

"She is," I'd reassure him.

I made that assertion long before that night when I got on the subway at Grand Central Station and stood next to the door with my back to the crowded car, because it was so full, and stared out into the tunnel, and my eye was caught by another train traveling alongside my train at the same speed and in the same direction, so close I thought it could easily crash, and suddenly, also standing at a door on the train right in front of me, I saw Reina looking at me. I would swear to it. We looked at each other for a few seconds, but who was counting? We both touched the windows with our hands, each his or her own, we turned pale, I scratched at my window, and she slowly opened her mouth as if to say something, maybe something beautiful, something even a little cheap like "I'll come get you in the spring" or something like that, but she didn't say anything, probably because she knew she wouldn't have time, she knew that before even getting my name out, the trains would separate, just like they did, in fact, each one on its own track and to its own destination, rumbling away in a rush.

I got off at the next stop, even though it wasn't mine, and ran back and forth without knowing where to go. I pulled at my hair and ears. I dug my nails into my lips and punched my fists into the walls. Maybe it's because I saw her and she got away that I let myself slip onto the floor and shouted as I hadn't since the day I arrived, hoping that my shout would catch up with her through the tunnels.

"You've been looking for her for so long, you're starting to see her," they told me.

"It's just your imagination."

"You were tired and you got confused."

"You were hallucinating, Marlon."

Nobody believed me, but it was her. When we see each other, she'll confirm it. And then we'll be able to laugh at our fear. I will tell her about how the following nights I took that same train at the same time, every day for two weeks, changing cars, getting out at every station, my eyes alert to everything the first few days, my eyes reddening after a while, after I got more upset and disappointed, like someone who has seen someone rise from the dead only to see her die again.

Reina's eyes lit up, one more than the other, but who could blame her? After all, she had just bought her dream.

"Everything has a price," Fabiola said as she took our money. "Sanqu bery mooch," she said after counting it.

But her price wasn't paid in full by the dollars we'd just given her. There was more to come.

"Pay close attention," Fabiola said with a smile.

Reina smiled also and leaned forward. That other woman, the one we called Caleña because she was from Cali, smiled at me and uncrossed her legs like the last time to show me that she wasn't wearing anything under her skirt that day, either. I could relax because Reina hadn't noticed. She was too focused on listening to Fabiola's instructions.

"We're not all going to travel together," she said. "We're going to split up into smaller groups."

"Are you coming with us?" someone asked.

"Of course not," Fabiola said. "I've got to manage everything from here, but someone from our organization will meet you there. Next week we're going to give you tickets: Medellín–

Bogotá–Panama–Guatemala City–Panama–Bogotá–Medellín. On each of your tickets you'll find your own travel date."

There was grumbling, chairs scraping, and several hands that shot up to ask questions.

"Why are you charging us for the return tickets?"

"Why are you splitting us up?"

"What are we going to do when we arrive?"

"Just a minute," said Fabiola with a big smile and a reassuring look on her face. "Calm down, I'll explain everything. If you can't show a return ticket, you'll have problems with Immigration in Guatemala and it's very likely they won't let you in. But we have a way for you to get your money back. When you reach the United States, mail your ticket to a family member, and we will reimburse you for thirty percent of its value."

Again there was grumbling and lots of questions—what do you mean? why don't we get all of it back?—and before she had a full-blown mutiny on her hands, she stood up, raised her voice, and said very firmly:

"You should be grateful that we're willing to give you anything back, because they don't at the other agencies. If anybody here wants to risk going with a one-way ticket, it's not my problem, but there's very little chance they'll let you in."

Everybody shut up. We all looked at each other. Caleña uncrossed her legs again, now more slowly so that I could see everything crystal clear—the most delicious temptation of hair and flesh together—but I kept a poker face, worried that Reina was going to discover us. Fabiola smiled again when she saw us sitting there in silence.

"I like to know we all agree," she said. "Now don't you worry, we won't separate those of you who want to travel together." Caleña looked right at me. "We're just trying to avoid sending a large group because that may look suspicious. Because, besides all of you here, there will be others from other cities.

Remember, we are a large, respectable organization, and people all over the country seek our services."

Next she warned us that now she was going to say something very important, and she began to talk about what we could and could not bring. Don't even think of bringing phone numbers, addresses, or names of people in the United States. Beware. You have to know everything—names, telephone numbers, and addresses—all by heart. You will bring a medium-sized suitcase, and inside that a smaller suitcase, and take note, only one change of clean clothes and another of black clothes. I repeat: Only one change of clothes and another of black clothes. No food, nothing for anybody else, not even a picture or a letter. In other words, leave even your memories behind.

"Does anybody have any questions?" Fabiola asked, but we were all paralyzed, and Caleña even closed her legs. That business about the black clothes reminded me of death and wakes. I saw Reina slowly raise her hand.

"What are the black clothes for?"

"You'll need them for the night we cross the border."

"How are we going to cross?"

"I still don't know. But no matter how, it's always better to wear dark clothes."

The whole thing sounded bad to me. I remembered what Carlitos had told me: They've killed a lot of people there, they catch them, rape the women, kidnap the children, many drown in the river. I'd already told Reina, but she answered me back: What, they don't kill people here? They don't rape here? They don't kidnap children here? I'd rather die trying, she said, than have them kill me here with my arms crossed and for no good reason. She always left me without arguments. What could I say in defense of a country where a tragedy was lurking around every corner, just waiting to put you into mourning?

"Why do we need such a big suitcase to carry so few things?" Caleña asked.

"To trick them," Fabiola explained. "You can't travel as tourists without any luggage, but as soon as you land in Guatemala, you're going to give your suitcases to our people and you'll just keep the smaller bag."

Everything seemed so simple, but that meeting left me with a bad taste in my mouth, like of something criminal. Add to that the stealing of the dollars, and I really started to feel like a felon. Fabiola set a date for the next meeting, but before we left, we chatted a little among ourselves. Reina grabbed my hand to keep me out of reach of Caleña, who kept looking at me craftily. I knew next to nothing about my traveling companions, only their destination, though we all shared the same fear and anxiety.

"It's the third time I enter," said a man whose name was Stalin, "and it's not because they've sent me back."

"So why do you keep going?"

"I like to travel. Anyway, with my name they'd never give me a visa."

He told us how he'd gone the two previous times with a different agency. The first time he crossed in a gas tank; they were like sausages in a can, he said, boiling hot because the desert is pure hell, and terrified because it was his first time. The second time he crossed the river on a tire, his ass soaking wet, he said, and even more afraid than in the gas tank because he didn't know how to swim. Now that he has more money, he's switched agencies. This one is much higher class, he added; they say it's much easier to cross over with them.

"What's the scariest part?" a woman asked.

"The scariest part is wherever there are police, and that's just about everywhere," said Stalin. "You've got to watch out for both the Mexican and the gringo police."

"What happens if they catch you?" the woman asked, and you could hear the trembling in her voice.

"Everything, anything," Stalin affirmed. "Anything can happen."

I wanted to keep listening, but Reina said, Let's go—whether she said it because she was afraid that Stalin's stories would make me back out or because Caleña had come up to listen and was standing right next to me, I don't know.

"Which eye do you look at?" Roger Pena asked me, and seeing me confused, he added, "Because you can't look at both at the same time."

"Sometimes one, sometimes the other," I told him.

"Which do you like better?"

"Well . . . I don't know."

"Reina has one Colombian eye and one gringo eye," Roger Pena pointed out, and he doubled over in one of his off-key laughing fits.

"What are you laughing at, Roger?"

"At us Colombians," he managed to say through his laughter. "So crass! Just imagine how pompous we are that we sing 'Happy Birthday' in English."

He kept laughing. I was left hanging, not knowing what the joke was about or why he had mentioned our "hapi berdi," as we pronounced it, and he kept laughing when it struck twelve and he turned off the light. He totally surprised me when he asked me in the darkness:

"How are you doing on clothes?"

"I'm sorry, Roger, but a while ago I stopped understanding what you were talking about."

"Oh, *niño*," he said irritably from his bed. "Do you need clothes?"

"Well, of course, Roger, that's something you always need."

"Tomorrow you're going to come to work with me."

I didn't ask him to explain, because he sounded tired. I would have to wait until the next day and allow myself to be lulled to sleep by the ball bouncing off the wall.

The sound of another ball woke me up very early. Roger had already gotten up and left the room, but I found him when I went to take a shower. He was carrying his little dog in his arms. Demon barked furiously at the poor old guy who wandered around the building at all hours of the day and night, but Roger didn't do anything to make the animal shut up.

"Demon was making pee-pee," he shouted over his barking. "Get ready, we've got to leave soon."

"Roger," I told him, "I don't have any money to spend on clothes, you know that."

"You're not going to spend any. It's on me."

I wanted to ask him what clothes had to do with his work, why he was going to buy me clothes just like that, since doing good deeds wasn't exactly up his alley. I had so many questions about Roger that by the time I got back to the room to get dressed, I decided to go back to the bathroom rather than change in front of him.

Before going out, Roger Pena looked at himself in the mirror to make sure that his long strands of hair were covering his bald spot. He picked up his dog in one arm and his bag in the other. Downstairs, Demon went off again when he saw the old man sleepwalking.

"What a strange man," I said to Roger as we were walking toward the station.

"He's an Achaean. We call him Father Dionysus."

"He's a what?"

"A Greek, you ignorant child. He's the oldest resident in the building, but ever since they built the club next door, he hasn't slept."

"Because of the bouncing of the ball?"

"I think it's more because he's angry."

"But he looks so calm," I told him. "He even looks like he's sleeping."

"Maybe he's a sleeping volcano," said Roger. "He'll soon either drop dead or explode."

Before we entered the subway station, Roger put Demon in the bag and gave him a kiss before closing the zipper. We got off the train at Lexington and walked to Bloomingdale's. I hadn't been in Manhattan more than three times; it wasn't my territory, and I preferred to observe it from far away, from that rooftop. I felt even less worthy of going into the shops: the prices and the people there made me feel like an alien, and it seemed like a waste of time to even look around. The closest I had ever come to Bloomingdale's was their bags that get passed around until they end up in some poor person's hands. But Roger Pena entered Bloomingdale's as if he knew it like the back of his hand and was used to doing all his shopping there. I followed behind him like a servant they take on vacation, cautious and overwhelmed, amazed at how Roger's behavior had suddenly changed, the way he was walking, how he looked through the racks of clothes, how he made eye contact with the other customers. He carried himself elegantly, almost pretentiously. He looked at the price tags and smiled, and the whole time I kept feeling like I had no business being there at all.

"Okay," he said to me, "what would you like?"

"No, Roger," I told him. "Look at the prices."

"Just pick something out and don't be an ass," he said under his breath.

Just so we could get out of there, more than anything else, I pointed to a shirt.

"Pick another one," Roger said.

I pointed to another one and then to a pair of pants. Roger picked up everything I chose and hung it over his arm with as much confidence as someone who is planning to pay.

"Now make sure no salespeople come near."

"What?!" I exclaimed, horrified.

"Don't shout," Roger said, calm and smiling. "Just keep your eyes wide open."

I definitely wanted to run, but I couldn't feel my legs under me. I wouldn't have been able to warn him that someone was coming, because I was hypnotized by Roger's slow and steady movements as he zipped open the bag and skillfully placed the clothes under Demon, who was calm and obedient and let Roger move him around like a dove trained for a magic act, all of this going on while Roger Pena's expert hands conjured up the disappearance of both the animal and the clothes, making me wonder if I was dealing with a magician or a thief.

The clothes fit me perfectly. I never could have had them if I hadn't gotten them that way. Not to mention, it was the first time I'd had anything new in the United States; everything else I had was crummy old hand-me-downs people had given me. Wearing new clothes made me feel like a new man, and I wasn't the only one who noticed.

"Check out how they're checking you out," Giovanny Fonseca said to me.

We were in Flushing and it was July 20, Colombian Independence Day. The air was full of exaggerated expressions of patriotism: flags, pennants, tricolor hats, colorful shawls, iguanas, boa constrictors, T-shirts that proudly displayed the red, yellow, and blue of the flag; God, the Fatherland, and Motherhood; *Yo quiero a Colombia*, and all the other patriotic shit anybody could think of. There were orchestras playing, food frying, motorcycles, native costumes, drunkards, and beauty queens; an entire party for the masses right in the middle of New York City.

I spent the whole time looking at every face and into the eyes of every woman, just in case I suddenly came across one with one eye darker than the other. I held conversations without looking at the person I was talking to, just in case the person I was looking for walked by at that exact moment I was distracted. That's why I thought Giovanny was talking to his wife and not to me when he said:

"Check out how she's checking you out."

Then I felt the blow on my arm and realized he was talking

to me and not to Gladys. So I looked over at the person who was supposedly looking at me, and to tell the truth I didn't see anybody in particular, but Giovanny kept pushing his mouth out in front of him like he was pointing, then he opened it along with his eyes to warn me:

"She's on her way over here, *hermano*."

One of the women wearing a Colombian flag came walking toward us with a big smile on her face. Her cheeks were painted with the red, yellow, and blue, and her hips were swaying as if she was the Fatherland herself and the party was in her honor. But I didn't need to see her costume to realize she was one of us Colombians: even though she was being flirtatious, she still had that guilty, apologetic look on her face, like all Colombians do, especially in foreign airports.

"Hi, Milagros," Gladys greeted her, and while they were kissing each other, Giovanny and I stood there looking at each other like two idiots. Then came the formal introductions: This is Giovanny, my husband, and this is Marlon, a friend of ours. She gave Giovanny a wink and greeted me with a long look; Hey, Marlon, she said, and continued looking at me even after she had said it.

She stayed with us, or, as Giovanny said later:

"She stayed with you," and then added, "You've already got it halfway in."

That afternoon, I saw her only as a delicious and cheerful woman who made me laugh and even got me dancing. But that night when I went to sleep, I was still thinking about Reina, not yet suspecting that soon there would be nights when I would go to bed thinking about somebody else; that the presence of Milagros Valdés in my life, like a set of timbales, a flight of parrots, New Year's Eve, or Carnaval, was reason enough to celebrate, and that just as her name indicated, she would work nothing less than a miracle.

I never thought that the day we'd meet would be a Sunday. The name of the day doesn't necessarily make any difference; the only thing that does matter is what can happen during it. But Sundays are merciless, and they can even decide how things are going to turn out, either for you or against you: his life was saved because it was Sunday and there wasn't any traffic so we got him to the hospital; or, it was Sunday so there was only one doctor on duty and he was taking care of other people and he had died by the time he got to him. However you cut it, Sunday is not a very good day. I prefer to ignore it and think that the day I see Reina won't have a name.

Maybe it's because it's Sunday that the bathrooms were full when I rushed off the bus, trying to be first in line. I had fifteen minutes to change my clothes, shave, eat breakfast, and call her. The instructions were clear: the bus will leave in fifteen minutes. I asked the driver what time he had so I could synchronize my watch. I even thought of the possibility that he'd play a dirty trick, change the time just to leave us behind. I changed clothes in three minutes, shaved in five, then bought breakfast—

hamburger, french fries, and a Coca-Cola. I wonder if this is the American breakfast, or *desayuno americano*, they offer in hotels in Colombia.

Reina didn't answer. I dialed very carefully, and again the machine answered: Hi, please leave your name and a message and I'll call you back. I could leave a message, tell her: Wait, I'm coming; but I don't want to have a machine as an intermediary. I want her to hear my real, live voice, even if I do sound kind of vague and empty like on the tape.

I was wearing clean clothes, but I'd shaved sloppily, and I had my breakfast in a bag when I got back to the bus with three minutes to spare. It didn't surprise me that I was the first to get on. The driver already had the motor running, and he asked me: What happened to your face? I cut myself shaving, I told him, 'cause I had to do it in five minutes. He made fun of me: Don't you get blood all over my bus, and began to honk furiously. Outside, the others who didn't want to be left behind in a town in the middle of nowhere ran to get on the bus.

"Are you with someone?" Milagros asked soon after we met.

"Yes," I answered.

She blushed, thinking she had flirted too boldly, given me too many lingering looks, just the fact that she had spent the whole day with me.

"But she's not here," I said, and since she didn't understand, I had to tell her my story, which already bored me because I had told it so many times. And since it was such a long story, I suggested we take a walk.

"I'll follow you," I said.

We walked slowly. She interrupted me only to say: Let's cross here. Wait for the light to change. Turn right here. I wasn't frightened at all as I let her lead me through the streets of Queens.

"Wherever I'm walking," I told her, "I always have the sensation of having been on that street before."

"On all except one," Milagros said after knowing my situation.

The street where I left Reina and where she is no longer. Now there is someone else in that little room, someone else trying to find out what he can scrape together in New York City.

"It wouldn't do me any good to find that building now."

"I bet you've never looked at the sidewalks at night," Milagros said.

When I walked I always looked at people's faces, or looked down at the sidewalk, but only to avoid stepping in the dog shit, that's why I'd never noticed that the sidewalks were sparkling.

"What makes them sparkle?" I asked her, amazed.

"They're full of ground diamonds," Milagros said, and laughed out loud when she saw my surprise.

"Really?"

"Of course, handsome," she said, and took my arm to keep walking, but I kept thinking of that "handsome" she had said and the look on Reina's face if she'd see me walking arm-in-arm with Milagros Valdés, who wanted to study music and sing salsa, make CDs and become famous.

"Like Celia Cruz," she said, and she began to sing and swing her hips.

That's why she was here and not in Los Angeles with her parents, or even back in her hometown, in Colombia's hottest region along the Caribbean coast, where they say the people dance more than they work.

"You might not believe it," she told me, "but this is where salsa is happening." Then she asked me, "What are your plans?"

She was talking about my life and what I was going to do with it: study, work, or nothing at all. But I had put off my decision until I found Reina. Then the two of us would decide what we were going to do with our lives, probably what almost anybody who can does with their life: first study, then work, then sit back and watch yourself get old. But when Milagros asked me, all I thought about was working to eat, pay for phone calls, and search for Reina in vain.

"Oh, handsome," she said again, "all this time cleaning toilets and collecting garbage. With your good looks, you could be a waiter or at least a busboy."

Again she took me by the arm, but the cheerful expression on her face had changed to one of slight disapproval. We walked a little farther in silence until I heard the roar of the subway.

"Does this station work for you?" Milagros asked. "You can get the number seven here."

I didn't want to say good-bye just like that. I wanted to say that it was wonderful to meet her, that I so much enjoyed walking in New York without being afraid, that I loved how she sang. So I decided to tell her, and I began to, but just then a train passed overhead, shaking the earth and drowning out my voice.

"Run, run," Milagros told me, "this one's going in your direction." She gave me a slap on the butt and blew me a kiss as I skipped up the stairs and shouted back:

"Call me at the restaurant! Let's get together again!"

The next day, Giovanny said to me: I don't know Reina, but that one is just the way my God likes to make them.

Giovanny rolled his eyes and rubbed his hands together. I held on stubbornly to the idea that Reina could not be replaced, that it was stupid to put somebody else in the place of someone who would, sooner or later, reappear.

"On top of that," Giovanny continued, "this one is here, and the other one is nowhere. And don't look at me like that."

"You'd do better to shut up, Giovanny."

He shut up, but only for a few seconds. He had a lot of questions and he wasn't going to hold them in.

"So tell me, what does Milagros do besides work miracles?"

I looked down and laughed.

"Why are you blushing?" Giovanny asked. "Tell me what happened."

"Nah, it's just that I showed her how ignorant I was," I said, and told him that I had asked Milagros what she did.

"She said she worked selling 'groserías.'"

And I, like an idiot, asked her:

"You mean in a sex shop?"

Milagros almost died laughing, so much so that she almost couldn't explain to me that she worked in a store that sold things to eat—groceries—not gross things, as I'd understood it.

"That didn't happen because you're ignorant," Giovanny told me, "but because you're a damn fool. If, instead of throwing your money away on phone calls, you'd enroll in an English class, you'd even be able to find yourself a better job."

"She told me she'd teach me," I told him.

Then I answered more of his questions and told him that Milagros wanted to be a singer, study music, and be famous. I told him that if serpents had hips they would move them like Milagros Valdés moves hers.

"What a woman!" Giovanny exclaimed.

"But I'm going to keep looking for her."

"For who?"

"Who do you think? Reina."

A few days later, as it turned out, Patricia took me to a woman who finds lost things.

"But Reina isn't a thing," I told her.

"If she can find a lost purse," Patricia explained, "why wouldn't she be able to find a girl?"

So we went to somebody named Madame Taylor, a witch who reads cards and other things and helped Patricia find everything she lost.

"Madame doesn't speak Spanish," she explained to me, "and she doesn't speak English very well, either. She's from somewhere over there, I don't know exactly where."

"So what am I going to do?"

"Don't worry, *hijo*, I can understand her."

Patricia told me that Madame asked her what she had lost now, and she said nothing, but that I had, and that Madame said that it didn't seem like I had lost anything, but from what she could see, I was the one who was lost.

"He lost his girlfriend, Madame."

Patricia explained the frightening expression on the woman's face.

"She says it's easier to find things, because things don't move on their own and people do."

Then she asked if I had something that belonged to the lost woman, and Patricia explained to her that I had arrived with barely my own shirt on my back. Then Madame shook her head and told Patricia that in this case it would be impossible.

"Tell her I have a picture of her," I told Patricia.

Madame kept talking in what sounded like gibberish, then she looked at the picture and shook her head and kept babbling.

"She says she isn't lost, that she can see beyond her own footsteps, that her different-colored eyes are like a chameleon's."

"But ask her where she is," I begged, "or if she thinks she can find her."

Madame Taylor dug her hand inside her fortune-teller's turban, scratched her head without taking her eyes off the picture, then dealt her cards out on the table. She asked me to choose ten cards at random, made strange noises come out of her mouth as she turned them over, then spoke in English with some kind of strange Slavic accent.

"She's not alone, and she's okay," Patricia translated. "She now has money, and she can't tell me exactly where she is because she's moved around a lot."

"But is she here in New York?" I interrupted.

"She could be, but she could also not be; this young lady is like the wind, she probably was born in February, and she, too, is looking for somebody."

"For me?!" I interrupted again.

"Could be and could not be. But anyway this girl isn't lost, and instead of looking for her, you should find yourself."

I looked at them totally confused, my heart was about to burst, my mouth was dry, and my throat was tight.

"What else?" I asked them.

Madame looked at the cards again and again shook her head, adjusted her turban, suddenly shoved her finger up her nostril, took it out, then spoke two words.

"What did she say?" I asked Patricia.

"Thirty dollars."

I turned white. I protested, asking Patricia how she could charge me so much for telling me so little, and it seemed like Patricia was translating my complaint to her because suddenly Madame turned into a viper: she swept the cards off the table and began to shout at me, even though she knew I couldn't understand a thing.

"I think you'd better pay her," Patricia told me. "I'll lend you the money."

We gave her the money and she stuffed it in her bosom, then she shooed me away like I was a fly, though she did say good-bye to Patricia and even smiled at her.

When we got outside, Patricia tried to comfort me, telling me that it hadn't been that bad, that at least I knew now that she was alive, and that she was probably looking for me. I wasn't convinced by any of it. I wanted to hear the name of a street or a city, get exact directions somewhere, something that would have given me back some hope, some motivation to keep looking for her.

Also, it upset me to realize that I, who don't even have a little bit of all that faith that keeps nuns going, for instance, had gone to look for Reina in some cards. And the only thing I got out of my visit to Madame Taylor was thirty dollars that were as lost as Reina.

In the seat where first Charlotte, then Gerardo—the Salvadoran who went to the bathroom and never came back—sat is now sitting a boy who doesn't stop staring at me. I don't look over at him in hopes that he won't speak to me, but anyway:

"What's your name?"

"Marlon."

"Where are you going?"

"Miami."

"Why?"

"To meet someone."

"Who?"

I turn to look at him with a stern expression on my face and say firmly: Someone.

"Is that why you look so weird?" he asks me.

At what precise moment did this little brat sit down next to me? I look at my reflection in the glass to see what is so weird about my face.

"You look like an idiot," the boy says to me.

I look around, trying to find his mother. A woman smiles at me from two rows back; they don't look alike, but she must have been the one to sit him down next to me.

"You want to play a game with me?" the boy asks.

"No."

"Why?"

"Because I don't."

"It's really easy," he says. "I think of something I am looking at and say the first letter, then you try to guess what it is."

"No," I repeat.

"*I,*" he says, beginning the game.

"Infanticide."

"No," he says. "You lose."

The days just before an escape go by very slowly, partly because, in addition to everything else, you are living in a state of despair that you have to hide. It was like this a few days before we left, the day Reina longed for and I was so scared of, even though it did mean that we would be together forever in New York. At some point Gonzalo said that Reina seemed very distracted lately. Who knows what she's thinking about, he said to me; and I repeated: Who knows, Gonzalo. Then he mumbled: She's so much like her mother.

I never talked to Gonzalo about how sacred New York was to Reina or about her plans. It was up to her to find the right moment to tell him. But Reina was a coward and never even looked for that moment. I insisted that she couldn't go away, just like that, without even leaving a note, like me, also a coward but less than her, who didn't tell him anything. The night before the trip she said good night to her father just like she did every other night, with a mechanical *hasta mañana* and a kiss repeated so often that it had lost all its meaning. Habit helped so that Reina's voice didn't shake, like my hand did while I was writing my good-bye note. It was just two or three lines telling them that I loved them, that I would miss them, that in case I never returned I hoped they would remember me affectionately. I rewrote it lots of times, my heart was pounding, and I was on the verge of crying; I tried to find words that would hurt less, that wouldn't show how insecure and how ungrateful I was. I walked slowly through the house like a first-time burglar who doesn't know what to steal, trying to decide where to leave the treacherous note. I tried the dining room, on the floor in front of the door to my parents' bedroom, taped onto the mirror in the bathroom, until finally, I don't know why, I left it on the heater. Maybe I secretly hoped that somebody half asleep would turn it on and the fire would burn up my lying words.

I didn't sleep that night, not so much because I had insomnia, but because I thought it would be the height of disrespect. I guess I'm not quite as hard-hearted as the murderer who manages to sleep peacefully the night before his crime. I slept like someone on death row, or someone who battles a mosquito all night long because its buzzing keeps him awake. When the alarm rang at five in the morning, my eyes were open, and even though I was wide-awake, it made me jump. I needed to lie there for a few minutes to get over the shock. I'd told everybody that I was getting up early that morning to play soccer with Juancho Tirado and the others, and they all looked at me strangely because I never played sports, much less in the early morning. But they weren't worried. They'd never have suspected that even I didn't have any idea when I'd be back.

It was still dark out when I went by to get Reina. She was waiting for me at the window, and when she saw me, she ran down the stairs and reached the street before I got to her door. She gave me a big hug, as if instead of us leaving together I had just arrived from far away. I carefully picked up her suitcase, put my bag with dark clothes inside it, looked at Reina's house one last time—feeling the same sorrow I felt when I looked at my own—and waited for her to give me the order I didn't want to obey.

"Let's go," she said finally.

Now I'm convinced that we really do have a lot of say about our own destiny. If I feel bad about anything, it's not about my bad luck, but about my own stupidity. To follow someone because you are in love with her seems to me now to be more about being foolish than about being honest or blind.

"Get off," I told Reina just as we were getting on the airplane.

"What happened?"

"Get off and step in first with your right foot."

It made me happy and made her smile at me. She knew about my apprehensions and my fears, not only about the airplane but also about what would be waiting for us once we arrived, but that step we took to get on the airplane was the first of a lot of very complicated steps we would be taking along the way. That's why it was meaningful, even if it's true that we still didn't know where my own steps would take me one day.

"We should probably check to make sure that the pilot didn't step in with his left," she said once we were in our seats. She said it with a smile on her face. She was trying to reassure me with a joke, but since it didn't work, she tried a kiss.

"No!" I pushed her away in confusion. "Remember what they told us."

That we should be sure not to do anything scandalous, nothing that would call attention to ourselves or make people look at us.

"She meant that for when we get there," Reina said.

"We'd better start watching what we do from now on," I told her. "Anyway, you know I don't like to be touched when I'm nervous."

It wasn't even fear: I just felt shattered. I was leaving everything and escaping like a criminal; and in the same way, I was going to enter the country that Reina had chosen. It wasn't only that the situation was terrifying; it also made me realize that there was no turning back. The whole thing and all the circumstances around it made me feel hurt and angry about a country that offered nothing besides blood and death and a future of poverty.

Reina squeezed my hand and said:

"In case it helps, I'm scared, too, even though it would be better if at least one of us was brave."

I felt like saying: Let's get off, Reina, we've still got time, but just as I was about to say that, the stewardess closed the door, the engines started up, and the airplane began to move backward. Then she said, with a knot in her voice and a tense smile on her face:

"We're outta here."

As the airplane taxied down the runway, I decided to look out the window one last time at the land I was leaving, and so that Reina wouldn't see me with tears in my eyes. We kept holding hands until we felt the full blast of the engines lifting us off the ground. Then I unlaced my hand and crossed myself and I saw her doing the same. Once we were in the air, I took Reina's hand again right away because I realized that she was crying, too.

Tell me more, she said. She wanted to know everything about my life, about me. We were in Central Park, surrounded by autumn trees, by the crazy and the rich of Manhattan. Why would anyone want to talk or hear about Panama?

"Then what happened?" Milagros asked.

She insisted, so I continued. We landed in Panama, really scared, even though we knew it was just a stopover, a change of airplanes, that the complicated part would begin in Guatemala, where we would have to go through Immigration. There were more than twenty of us, I think, because I only recognized the ones from Medellín. Caleña was there, too, the one I told you about who never stopped staring at me.

I was very nervous; every time a policeman passed by us, my foot would start to shake. At the last meeting, once Fabiola had all the money and could start talking about the risks, she warned us:

"You've got to watch out for the police; they're going to be your biggest problem," she said in a very serious voice but still with that mysterious smile.

Reina told me: Calm down, man, we're not doing anything wrong, wipe that guilty look off your face. But I couldn't help feeling panicky every time I saw one of them walk by us at the airport. I relaxed when I heard the boarding call.

"Why Guatemala?" Milagros asked. "Why didn't you fly directly to Mexico?"

To get into Mexico, we would have needed a visa, and they never would have given us one because of how broke we were. Somehow they got us visas for Guatemala, don't ask me how. We were supposed to sneak into Mexico, but we still didn't know how. When we got to Guatemala, we had our first big scare: the Immigration officer looked at us very suspiciously and asked a bunch of questions; but I kept quiet and let Reina do all the talking. She acted very flirtatious and explained to the man that we were tourists and were going to visit the Tikal pyramids. She showed him the return ticket, and she said: Don't worry, sir, we wouldn't give up our country for anything in the world.

I stopped talking for a few moments, but Milagros pushed me to go on.

Well, anyway, in the airport we were greeted by a dwarf with a sign that read PARADISE TRAVEL.

"A dwarf?" Milagros asked.

Well, almost. He was about an inch too tall for a dwarf, even though his voice sounded like he was over six feet tall. He acted like an army sergeant. He divided us up into two groups and sent us to two different hotels. He also asked us for money, dollars, because we were going to need some local money, and he said we should give him dollars so that he could change them into quetzales. A while later he came back and handed us some bills we'd never seen and sent us on to the hotel. While we were registering, I looked at a sign with the exchange rates and said to Reina: That dwarf cheated us. But she didn't seem to care; she just said that whatever he lacked in height he made up for as a thief.

Milagros hid her reaction to Reina's comment by quickly covering her mouth with her hand.

That was nothing, I told her. When we got to the room, we found two other people, two men who were traveling with Paradise Travel, too, and they'd already taken over the only two beds in the room. "What are you doing here?" Reina asked them, placing her hands firmly on her hips.

"That's what I was going to ask you," one of them said, quickly sitting on the bed.

We went down to the lobby and they told us that's how things were, that the agency had paid the hotel for four guests to a room, that we should be patient and they would bring two cots up to the room. Reina was furious: I'm not going to sleep on a cot, she said, and I'm not going to put up with their snoring and farting, either.

"Well, Miss Queen Bee, if we bother you that much, you'll just have to pay for another room."

Then came the shouting match. Thc guy at the receptiou desk said to us: If I were you, I wouldn't make such a fuss. I had to calm Reina down, even though what I really wanted to do was stand up for her. I was dying to be alone with her, but I knew how much it would cost to get a room for just the two of us. I told her it was for one night and that we were so tired we'd fall asleep right away anyway. We'd put the cots together and that would be that, I told her, and finally she gave in; but until she fell asleep, she was at it with those two, because they'd left the bathroom dirty, because they turned on the television, because they were walking around the room in their underpants.

"Well, they told us not to bring anything . . . ," one of them said as an excuse.

The next day, the telephone rang very early. It woke the three of us up, but Reina was already showered and dressed. She picked up the phone.

"Get ready," she said to me, ignoring the other two. "They're about to pick us up."

Actually they gave her detailed instructions: We should leave the big suitcase in the lobby and pack the fewest possible items in the smaller bag. Once we were ready and in the lobby, the dwarf called again and said that he wouldn't be able to pick us up, that we should take a taxi and make our own way to the airport.

Milagros got distracted watching two people go by on Rollerblades as if they had wings on their feet. It was getting dark and the air was getting cold.

"How about we get going, Milagros?" I suggested.

"And your story?" she asked, disappointed.

"There's lots of time to tell you it."

Milagros rolled over and lay on her back, looking up at the orange and blue sky.

"Someday when you least expect it, you'll find her, and nobody will ever see you again," she said.

I didn't tell her, so as not to give her false hope, that this least-expected day seemed to fade more and more as I got more worn out and I had less and less motivation. With every day that passed, I spent less time looking for Reina, partly because I had fewer places to look for her.

"Let's go and I'll tell you more on the way," I told her.

While we walked toward the subway, and later, hanging on to the bars in the train car, I told her that we left Guatemala on a broken-down bus and without the dwarf, not toward the Tikal pyramids, but northward, toward the Mexican border, that we drove through poverty and mountains that reminded me that we were still far away from the United States, because what we were seeing was our misery, the same Latin American landscape, the same movie that plays all the way from Mexico to the South Pole.

We were being tossed around by the swaying of the train and were crowded in with all the other passengers who'd also gone out that Sunday to treat their eyes to the wonders of Manhattan, and Milagros listened as I told her how just as night fell the bus reached a small town in the middle of nowhere, and how the man who met us led us into the jungle where we walked for an hour until we reached a hut, went inside, and waited for others who were supposed to arrive, and that when they heard the password, they were going to take us to the border.

At midnight three men showed up and told us that the route was being watched and that we'd have to wait until dawn. They also asked us for money to pay off the guards; it hurt to do it, but we took out our roll of bills and gave a few to the coyotes. They came back and led us out of the hut so the mosquitoes could devour us while we walked toward the river; it was almost dawn. There, they gathered us all together and ordered us to throw into the river our passports and any other documents that would identify us as godforsaken Colombians. People shouted in protest and there were threats of mutiny and suggestions that we turn back, but that alternative looked even grimmer, so we did as we were told; we threw our documents into the river as if we were tossing flowers into the grave of a loved one, and we watched them lovingly until we saw them sink.

Milagros pressed herself against me and said: Poor Marlon. Poor all of us, I told her. We had to get into some broken-down canoes, no more than four in each or we'd sink, and we rowed up the river, hugging the riverbank, to who knows where. About half an hour later they told us to get out and walk—it was already day—to a town called San Gregorio.

"I remember that place," I told Milagros, "because Caleña, dressed as usual like a prostitute, went right down on her knees and prayed."

I don't know if she was thanking the patron saint or asking him for help with what was coming, because even though we were already in Mexico, we still had half the madness left to go.

"I'll tell you the rest later."

The train stopped and Milagros had to get off at that station. Very reluctantly she said: Too bad we don't both get off here. I didn't know whether to blame her or thank her for making me tell her my story. I felt tired and relieved at the same time, as if I'd just made love.

"How long has it been since you've gotten any, kid?" Roger Pena asked me.

I answered him with a stupid smile, but Roger insisted:

"Abstinence is bad for the soul. One of these nights we're going to the whores."

"I don't have money to pay for one, Roger."

"Bah," he said. "Money is a woman's excuse. As Ovid said a long time ago, 'The sense of pleasure in the male is far more dull and dead than what you females share.'"

He suggested that in the meantime we go get ourselves more clothes. They do care how we look, Roger Pena admitted, and we agreed to go to Macy's the following morning.

The routine was the same as usual: Take Demon out to pee, give him nothing to eat, get him riled up by seeing Father Dionysus as we leave the building, then put him in the bag right before we get on the subway. We didn't talk on the way. I had the impression that Roger had gotten up on the wrong side of the bed. As we entered Macy's, he repeated the instructions, but this time he reminded me not to choose garments that were too bulky.

"That's the problem with winter clothes," he said.

But that was what I needed: I was already getting pretty uncomfortable in the cold. Roger told me I should make sure it would fit into the bag before choosing something. After looking around for a while I picked out two shirts.

"Shirts again?" Roger asked. "Don't you need any underwear? If you're going to sleep with that girl, you'd better be well outfitted," Roger Pena added jokingly.

We went to the underwear section, and Roger walked over to what he had in mind for me. Calvin Klein drives women crazy, he said as he held up a pair of underpants. What size are you? he asked, looking at my ass.

"I don't want to get Milagros's hopes up, Roger."

"She's already got them up."

He stuffed the underpants quickly into his bag, then went to the other side to look for mufflers. He picked out two and explained: One is for me. Abracadabra, he said, and they disappeared. He hadn't given me the signal, but I could tell we were done. We were already on our way out when we heard a voice behind us:

"Excuse me, sir."

Roger pretended it wasn't meant for him. Keep walking, he told me, but the man behind us insisted: Hey, you two. So we stopped and Roger turned around to confront the booming voice.

"Run, Roger," I whispered.

"Shut up and leave it to me," he said, as a rather large African-American man approached us.

I thought that I'd never go to jail, that instead I'd die right there from fear, caught in the act. I didn't hear or understand, and I don't remember much about the uproar that followed, but it was obvious the guard asked Roger to open the bag and Roger refused, and then the guard insisted on seeing what Roger had inside. Later Roger told me that he whined and protested until the guard grabbed the bag and started opening the zipper, at which point Demon, magically transformed into a ferocious beast, poked his head out. On top of the dog's furious barking, Roger started crying hysterically: I can't leave him alone, I always have to have him with me; you people are so intolerant, that's why I have to hide him.

The guard was terrified and dropped the bag and the dog on the floor. Demon looked like he was about to devour everyone, even his owner, and a couple of salespeople approached and told Roger that they didn't allow animals in the store; finally he was able to pick up the bag, even though Demon would continue his show until Roger ordered him to stop, but not until he dragged me out and shook me and shouted at me that everything was over.

I couldn't talk the rest of the day. I couldn't get over my fear, because I carried it around with me the way Roger Pena carried his dog. It was that old fear that has been pushing on my heart, squeezing it, ever since that day I went out alone, and I'm sure the fear will keep squeezing until I see her face-to-face and in the flesh, or until I get back to my own country, or until the day the fear itself just does me in. That morning in Macy's, it wasn't that I just had a fright; it was more like a mirror was being held up to me and I could see reflected in it what's always inside me: fear taking over the body of Marlon Cruz.

Clouds are covering the sun, and Florida isn't dazzling like in the pictures at tourist agencies. It feels like the sun is about to set right in the middle of the day. Darkness shouldn't bother me as long as I carry the sun inside of me.

"Your foot is shaking," says the boy sitting next to me.

"What?"

"I said your foot is shaking, like this." The boy imitates the tremor in my leg and laughs maliciously.

It's not only my foot: my whole being is trembling, and I wouldn't be surprised if the earth started trembling, like it did when Caleña told me that she'd found her. Or maybe the real miracle was that I'd found Caleña.

"Let's go to the whores—," Roger Pena proposed.

"Hey, Roger, man, you know I—"

"Don't interrupt me. Off we go. It's on me."

I agreed to go with him out of a feeling of gratitude. We're going to see some naked *colombianas*, he said on the way, and at the corner of Junction Boulevard he took me into a grungy striptease joint called Buga. The name was pure Colombian, but the blue-toned women in the pictures outside inviting you in, concealing only what their two hands could cover, were pure gringa. Nothing like the ones Roger Pena had imagined for his purposes.

"But I thought you didn't like *colombianas*?" I asked him.

"No, I don't like them," he repeated, "but they're the poorest and the most miserable, so they're also the cheapest."

The place was more squalid inside than out, a minihell, a showcase of the worst we've got, and the women were a whole different ballgame from the ones on the posters outside.

"Here you'll see a little of everything," Roger told me. "Mafiosos, guerrillas, kidnappers, whores, priests . . ."

In my surprise, I blurted out a stupid question: What are they doing here?

"What do you mean, what are they doing here?" Roger Pena shot back at me. "The same they do there: trafficking, kidnapping, extortion, whoring."

"Here, in the middle of New York City?"

"In New York and anyplace else they put us," said Roger.

We sat at the bar in front of the stage where the women were dancing naked. An extremely skinny woman took her leave of the miserable audience, and Roger ordered a beer for each of us. He warned me:

"Don't get into a conversation with anybody. You never know what you'll get yourself involved in."

I looked around to check out the hot scene at Buga. As usual, I asked myself what I was doing there, risking my life among the condemned.

"Look," Roger said to me, "that one is really sucking it up."

There, on top of us, snaking around indecently in a sequined bikini, was Caleña.

"I know her," I told Roger in a state of shock.

"Who is it?" he asked with a dry laugh. "Your sister or what?"

I quickly explained to him that this woman, without really doing anything, had been a thorn in Reina's side ever since the first meetings we attended in Medellín.

"I didn't know she was coming to New York. Whenever anybody'd ask her, she'd answer 'We'll see.'"

"Well, here she is," Roger pointed out, "and she's hot."

"I thought she'd stayed in San Antonio with the coyote."

Caleña took off her top. Her tits popped out like two springs and were greeted with a unanimous round of applause. I didn't know whether to stay or to leave. Caleña danced to the other side of the stage, where a couple of jerks were calling her over to them with dollar bills. Caleña shook the sequins on her ass in their faces.

"I think it's better if she doesn't see me, Roger."

"Why? She's the one who's naked, not you."

Under the shower of dollar bills, Caleña began to lower the only thing she had on. I watched from behind as the curve of her buttocks first appeared. When I saw her start to turn around, I shut my eyes. Then I heard whistles and catcalls and applause, and I felt Roger's mouth in my ear saying:

"You can open your eyes now, kid."

I opened them and saw Caleña's legs arching in front of my face; I lifted them and saw her clean-shaven cunt smiling a crooked smile, the smile of a *bandido*, the same way its owner would smile whenever she'd say to me: It's my pleasure, my love.

I thought: What would Reina say if she saw me now with my nose almost buried in that crotch, if she saw me in this hell-hole surrounded by ruffians, roughnecks, and troublemakers? Wouldn't she wonder, like I do, if it was worth doing everything we did so that we could leave everything we hated and after eating so much shit come and find the same old shit again?

"I'll be right back," Roger Pena told me, and he walked off behind a swaying ass.

The stage was empty but still lit by red lightbulbs. I took a sip of my beer, wondering if I should go find Caleña, but just then I felt some greasy hands over my eyes.

"Caleña?" I asked.

I turned around and she planted a couple of kisses on my cheeks in greeting. Holding on to my hands, she took a step back to look at me, and I noticed she was actually dressed.

"Where's the Fury?"

She let out a laugh when I told her that Reina had gotten lost, or rather that I was lost.

"What do you mean? Tell me all about it, my love."

This time I made it very brief since Caleña herself had been there for a big part of it; but unlike everybody else who'd heard the story, Caleña was laughing her head off while she listened.

"Oh, my precious, you must forgive me," she said, wiping away her tears of laughter. When she'd pulled herself together again, she asked me:

"And what are you doing now with that old faggot?"

I looked around for Roger Pena, but he had vanished in the horde. I'm renting a bed in his room, I explained to Caleña, and she answered: What a waste! Then she said: If I were you, I'd keep one eye open while I slept.

"And you," I asked her, "where do you live? Are you living alone?"

"Alone?" she exclaimed. "What, you think I'm ugly or something, my love?"

"You still with the coyote?"

"Him? He took me as far as his gasoline lasted."

She came closer, almost rubbing up against me, and with a sweet, sugary look in her eyes and tone in her voice, she said: What you saw just now, I've been saving it for you for a long time. She grabbed my crotch, which was all shriveled up, and stuck her tongue down my throat. She didn't taste like honey, as I'd expected, but more like rum. She looked at me silently; we were both quiet. I think Caleña saw in my eyes the proof that I was the one who was lost, not because I didn't know where I was, because now I could find my bed, but because she saw me as one of those lost souls who has mortgaged his existence to another's will. Caleña knew it back then, after those first meetings, she knew it by my secretive glances; I didn't need New York or the night or the labyrinth to lose myself. All she had to do was look in my eyes to realize that one day I would get lost in my own house. That's why she said:

"We've got to find the Fury."

Among my collection of bad memories, one of the worst is the trip from the Guatemalan border to Mexico City. It was the only time I said to Reina: I'm going back. Go on, she told me, and crossed her arms over her chest, then added: I'll continue on my own. Reina alone and with her arms crossed, dirty, exhausted, so vulnerable in that savage place. Try to understand me, Reina, I told her, and she snapped at me: What is it you want me to understand?

We had already lost count of the hours we'd spent on that bus, talking as little as possible so that nobody would notice from our accents that we were Colombians. You can't be a Colombian outside of Colombia, and even inside Colombia it's complicated to be Colombian, as if it was something that kind of made you sick all the time. But we didn't need to talk to admit that we were defeated, that none of what was happening to us was what they'd promised.

"I'll continue on my own," Reina repeated. She was sitting down and I was standing because we had only one seat between us. I squatted and rested my head on her lap. I can't take it anymore, I whispered, and she said with her mouth close to my ear: When it's over, we'll forget all about this. I kissed her thighs even though I knew that I'd carry these bad memories with me to my grave.

At that moment we heard the sound of something falling. It was our bag, which we'd put on the luggage rack a little ways behind our seat because the racks overhead were full. But it didn't just fall by itself; somebody had thrown it down and put another one in its place.

"What's going on?" Reina said in a challenging voice as she turned around.

"That bag was in my place," shouted an old Indian woman whose face was so weathered you could hardly tell her age or her sex.

And we were off and running. Reina claimed that the seats and the racks weren't numbered, and the other one said that it was logical that the rack belonged to the person sitting below it. Reina threw her bag on the floor and put ours back up, and the other threw ours off and put hers up, and it went on like this until everybody was getting involved. The people traveling with us took our side, but when Reina and the Indian woman were about to come to blows, the driver slammed on the brakes and stomped back to the epicenter, shouting, not to calm things down, but rather to give us hell.

"Aha!" he exclaimed. "Foreigners. How nice. I bet you're all just tourists."

He asked us to get off the bus for a moment, only the tourists, he said laughing; once outside he told us that the *federales* were very upset about all the bad things people were saying about them, so they were insisting that the laws be strictly enforced. Of course, I'm sure you people have all your papers in order, he said, because if I'm wrong, it would be a very hard job for me to convince those snitches that I'm not carrying any chickens, as we call illegals like you, on my bus.

So, in order to save him all that work, we had to give him money. It wasn't easy to agree on an amount. At the same time, the other passengers were putting on the pressure, shouting insults at us, suggesting that we should just let our women fight it out. When we got back on the bus, we didn't even have our one seat to share or a place to put our very small bag.

Now I'm traveling with only a few things more than I had before, but I shouldn't forget that I arrived in New York with only the shirt on my back, and the little I have is what I've managed to collect over the year, which seemed to go on forever. I also have the letters my friends sent me, others from my parents, pictures of me with Giovanny, Patricia and Don Pastor, and the guys at the restaurant. I didn't bring any pictures of me with Milagros because I didn't want to have to give any explanations, and I didn't want anybody to think that I ever considered the possibility of replacing Reina. I also brought the clothes I stole with Roger Pena. Some other junk got lost when we had to rush out of the room, that early morning when Father Dionysus went crazy.

"What was that?" Roger Pena said, waking up with a start.

"What was what?"

The balls had stopped bouncing, and the silence was as deafening as a scream. The two of us sat up in our beds to listen.

"You can't hear anything," Roger said. Then he asserted, "Something's wrong."

"Let's wait," I suggested. "Maybe they've just left."

"No. When they take a break, it doesn't sound like this."

A moment later there was other noise, this time not through the wall, but from down below in our own building. It reached our door very quickly, as if it had climbed up with the elevator.

"What's going on?" Roger asked the people out in the hallway through the closed door from his bed.

"Let's turn on the light, Roger," I suggested.

"Shhhh!"

I heard him running toward the door and opening it, and then the hall light struck me in the eyes. I shut them, then heard:

"Father Dionysus killed two."

Two men, unfortunately for them, had come to the club at dawn to play racquetball and just as they'd finished the first set, they saw Father Dionysus on the other side of the glass in his bathrobe and holding a gun; before they could even wonder what that strange apparition was, the Greek was pumping them full of bullets.

"Quick," Roger ordered. "We've got to get out of here."

He was rushing around the room, but I couldn't see him. Demon started barking.

"Turn on the light, Roger."

"In five minutes this building is going to be full of cops," he said.

"Turn on the fucking light, Roger!"

When he turned it on I saw that he was rushing to pack up Javier's clothes and had one suitcase of his own ready, and the dog was in its bag.

"If you don't leave now, you'll have to attend to our guests," he told me.

"Where are we going?" I asked him while I was trying to pack up my things.

"I shall rush out as I am, and walk the street with my hair down, so."

"What are you talking about, Roger?"

"Me, nothing. It was Eliot who said that."

The first sirens were blaring but were still pretty far away. Roger got frantic, picked up his dog, and pushed the suitcase with his foot toward the door.

"You haven't paid me for the week," he said.

By the time I turned around to tell Roger I would pay him on Friday, he was gone. I could hear the sirens much closer now, so I grabbed whatever I could carry and rushed out. People were stampeding through the halls, everybody at different stages of dress or undress. They were all running down the stairs with anything they'd managed to grab. I assumed Roger would be out in the street, waiting for me to decide where we would go, but when I stepped outside, the lights of the patrol cars had already reached the corner, and just like that first time, I took off running, but this time I followed the crowd, trying to find Roger Pena in the middle of all that confusion.

Five blocks later, there was nobody with me; everyone had dispersed like jets of water from a broken faucet. There I was, again, alone in the middle of the street as if the asphalt was my destiny, and even though at any moment I could have panicked and tripped over my own feet, I knew that this escape was different because now I knew exactly where my steps were taking me. I was going straight to where I knew I would find Milagros Valdés.

She greeted me with the kind of delight you greet good news with, even though her relatives were much less pleased to see me. I'm not bringing my lover here; it's just that he doesn't have anywhere to go, I heard her say. Then she invited me in, and I followed her swaying hips into her room, where she said to me: This is your room; and I protested: No, Milagros, I'll sleep in the living room while I look for something else; but she insisted: Why look for something if you've already found it, love? And even though her hair was mussed from lying on her pillow and her eyes were swollen from sleep, I thought: This woman is a treasure; but anyway I said: I'll just stay for a while, then I'll go to Giovanny's.

"When one queen dies, another gets crowned," Giovanny said to me when I arrived at his house later that morning.

"Reina still reigns," I told him.

"She does?"

"Reina is alive."

Anybody who expressed any doubts always got the same strident answer: Reina is somewhere. That's also what I told Milagros, but in a gentler tone of voice because she didn't deserve harsh words. Milagros, I said to her, you know what I'm going to tell you.

"She showed up," she said, growing pale.

"No, but one day she will."

A song was playing on the radio that talked about somebody lost in dreams. I thought that Milagros would turn it off right away, but she hummed softly: I'll look for you flying in the sky, and then she said:

"I'll take my chances."

It was me who couldn't decide what card to play with her. I rejected her caresses, changed the subject whenever she tried to talk about us, about the two of us as if we were one, and even though we saw a lot of each other, I never went past her door, and then I'd go on to sleep at Giovanny's.

"When are you going to come in?" Milagros asked me.

"Your family doesn't like me," I offered as an excuse.

"It's none of their business."

"Let's keep walking and I'll tell you more," I proposed, and she followed me even though she wasn't very happy about it.

I began telling her about how before we arrived in Mexico City, we had to change buses in Oaxaca because the tickets the dwarf bought us were only good to there, and by the time we arrived in Oaxaca, we were already damaged goods. One guy in our group, an older guy with a big mustache that made him look Mexican, went up to the ticket window and with his Colombian accent bought everyone tickets to Mexico City. The rest of us preferred not to talk, not even to ask for help. We had to wait a while, but it was worth it, because we all got seats on that bus. Before getting on, one of the people in our group told us to keep an eye out as we approached Mexico City, because everything was so big and beautiful, and Caleña, taking advantage of a short lapse in Reina's vigilance, approached me and whispered in my ear: I bet you've got things even bigger and more beautiful.

"What nerve!" Milagros exclaimed.

But neither Reina nor I saw anything. I think neither of us even realized that we'd gotten to Mexico City because we'd both fallen asleep the second the bus started up, and even though the road was winding and the bus was braking and jerking around, we didn't see or feel anything until we got woken up by everybody struggling to get off the bus. Great, I thought, at last we're in a big city, but what I didn't know was that the bigger the city, the bigger the problems, and it wasn't until we got to the hotel they had assigned to us, a hotel that stood about as straight as the Leaning Tower of Pisa, that we realized they'd lied to us again.

"Yes," said the receptionist, "you all have reservations." We all cheered until she asked, "How would you like to pay? Cash or credit card?"

At that moment, any one of us would have killed the dwarf, Fabiola, or anybody else who identified themselves as belonging to the "organization." There were cries and shouts and a lot of swearing, and somebody suggested that we take up a collection to call Paradise Travel in Medellín and complain about this string of abuses and lies. But who was about to spend the little we had left on fighting and complaining when anyway we were going to have to pay for that night and probably many more? In other words, nobody signed on. Everybody decided to hold off our attack on Fabiola until we got north, where, supposedly, we'd see everything in a rosier light.

That night we slept four to a room again, but this time Reina didn't make a fuss and just lay down next to me, sensibly and quietly; I got the feeling that this woman who'd always reigned had finally been defeated.

"We're almost there" was the only thing she said, her words so slurred I thought she was talking in her sleep.

They woke us up at dawn, everybody at the same time, to tell us to go immediately to the airport and buy tickets to Monterrey, that they were waiting for us there to take us to the border that same night.

Most of us met down in the lobby, but some didn't even show up. By now the group was in total chaos: Let's go back; let's go to the embassy; but there's no money; we're too exhausted; we can't go on. Everybody was giving their opinions at the same time; everybody was only interested in saving his own skin. We're not a group anymore, I thought.

"A ticket to Monterrey is cheaper than one to Colombia," Reina said over everybody else's voices.

"We don't have any money left," some said. "We'll have to stay here until we can get more."

Reina took me aside and said: We've still got enough; then she turned and announced to the others:

"We're going."

"Me, too," Caleña said. Reina was about to say something to her, but she held her tongue when she saw that four other people were joining us, too.

So, Milagros, that morning we arrived in Monterrey, bathed and rested and with more hope than fear, though there was always fear. We were met there by a contact, and when we complained to him, he told us that he was a freelancer, that we would have to take our complaints back to our own country. Nobody brought it up again because everything we had to do had to be done quickly: Get on a bus that would take us to Reynosa in two and a half hours; there we'd find a hotel where we'd spend that night and wait for instructions to pass, finally, over the border into the United States.

Reina, Monterrey, Reynosa—it was all so monarchic, so royal. We were almost out of money, and I couldn't stand the thought of everything repeating itself: again a hotel and a room full of people, hot and stinking like a jail cell, because Reynosa was an oven, and anyway they didn't let us go out, Don't you dare let them see you in the streets. All we did was wait for the telephone to ring, but it didn't ring that night or the following day. Reina blew up when she came out of the bathroom, furious because the toilet was clogged with shit and toilet paper, but even more furious when she saw me blowing on Caleña's neck.

"You going to get it on with her right here in front of everybody, or what?"

"She was hot, Reina, and she asked me to do her a favor."

"Can't get me pregnant blowing on my neck, Reinita," Caleña told her.

Reina's foot jerked forward like she was about to kick her, but instead she rushed out and I followed her: Don't go out, Reina, remember what they told us; but she ran down the stairs in a rage and told the person in charge:

"Give me a room for two."

"Reina, there's no need."

She paid for the night in advance, then went upstairs to the room, took a shower, and without saying a word, just like I wasn't there, got into bed and went to sleep or pretended to go to sleep; in any case she went to bed that night without talking to me . . .

"Aha!" Milagros exclaimed.

"What do you mean?"

"You got quiet."

"I'll tell you the rest later, Milagros. I'm a little tired."

I didn't want to tell her more, because it wouldn't have been appropriate. Milagros would never hear about the following morning, very early, when I was woken by a hand on my chest. It was Reina's hand caressing me, up to my shoulders and through my hair. Then there were two hands, and then Reina on top of me, rubbing herself against me, touching me passionately, hot because Reynosa was burning and so was she. So hot that soon she had taken off all her clothes and then took off mine. She smiled when she saw my hard, hot joy, she took it in her hands and sucked on it slowly, as if it was an ice cream cone that would cool her off. Then she slid up my body, leaving kisses planted all along the way, and finally reached my mouth, passing on to me the taste of my own sex still in her saliva, grabbed it firmly and slowly shoved it inside her, closed her eyes, opened her mouth just a little tiny bit, and moaned in time to her movements. I added my moans to hers. It was very hot in Reynosa.

They didn't call us the whole next day, so we didn't go out. We stayed in the room paying off the debt that we'd been accumulating since Medellín, all day naked, sweaty, stinking, but as happy as if we were screwing in New York.

"We're going to keep going in New York," I told Reina.

"New York," she whispered, and opened her legs for me to go inside her again.

We didn't stop because we got tired, but because we got a call at midnight. It was the guides who had come to get us. They wanted us to put on our dark clothes and be ready immediately. While we were getting dressed, Reina and I looked at each other. Without saying a word, we both knew we were about to take the final leap, and just like cats, we'd have to land on our feet.

The earth had swallowed up Roger Pena and his mangy mutt. Father Dionysus was arrested: he had killed the two men because they didn't let him sleep, he declared to the newspapers.

"But he always looked like he was asleep," I commented to Milagros.

"The noise was his nightmare," she said.

"I hope he can sleep in jail."

I also found out that, just like Roger Pena, his name wasn't what we called him. His name was Kostas Papadionissiou, he was sixty-two years old, and he had lived in New York for thirty years.

"Just imagine," Milagros said to me, "if I married you, for example, my name would be Milagros Cruz, and everybody would think I was related to the great Celia."

Then Milagros clammed up because I didn't say or do anything. Then she said:

"It was just an example."

I didn't tell her that the problem was me, not the example,

that in other circumstances I would have entered her house and all the rest like I should have, like she wanted, like she deserved.

"In my opinion, you're a faggot and you've got your head up your ass," Giovanny told me.

"Marlon is loyal," Patricia defended me.

"Loyal to what?" Don Pastor asked, and I understood perfectly what he really meant by his question.

That night, after closing up, I asked Giovanny to come with me to Buga to see Caleña. I'm not going for what you think, I told him. I need to talk to her, and he answered: All power to you, *hermano*, if you can talk to a woman with no clothes on.

We did, in fact, find her naked, twisting around on the stage. I preferred to wait for her in the dressing rooms, but when I asked a fat woman in a black bikini where they were, she spit in my face in a burst of laughter and said to me: Dressing rooms?! Oh, my beauty, you'd think we were on Broadway.

While Caleña finished sweeping the stage with her butt, I told Giovanny my latest worry.

"You know how long I've been cleaning toilets?"

"Since you lost yourself, or since you appeared. Or, in other words, since you appeared lost."

"And all indications are that Don Pastor has no intention of moving me out of there."

Three weak rounds of applause marked the end of Caleña's show. She passed by us as she was counting her three measly dollars. She greeted me with a kiss on the lips and my friend with a handshake, as if she really was a diva. I'll be out in a second, sugar, I'm just going to throw something on.

"What am I going to do, Giovanny?"

"Here, you can do anything you want," he told me, "with a flick of your hand." He pointed with his mouth to the fat woman who was taking her tits out under a reflecting mirror. Then Caleña appeared and went straight to the heart of the matter.

"If you've come to look for your queen, there's no news, but if you've come for me, I'm ready and willing."

She grabbed my hand and led me over to a table. My *macho* is out of town, she said, and you can't believe how horny I've been these days. She ordered beers for all of us.

"I've got to go," Giovanny said. "Gladys brings out the heavy weaponry after midnight."

Caleña ordered three beers anyway. I'll drink them, she said, to cool myself off. I asked her: Not even a clue? Not a one, sweetheart, she answered.

"And I'm looking for work, Caleña."

I said I needed to get out of the toilets and earn a little more money, or at least find work that was a little more stimulating.

"Stimulating?" Caleña asked flirtatiously.

I'm serious, I said, something Reina wouldn't be ashamed of when she does show up, an occupation Milagros won't have to hide from her family. Something, anything, Caleña, that will give me the courage to remain in New York.

"If you haven't made any money, it's because you haven't wanted to," she told me. "Here Colombians can make lots of money if they take advantage of their bad reputation."

All you had to do was look around at the clientele of Buga to understand what Caleña was talking about. Here we didn't need to talk under our breath about these things.

"I can help you."

She told me it was possible to go to bed poor and wake up rich: there are opportunities on every street corner in New York City.

"My man made me a promise."

He had told her: One night we'll go to bed in Queens and wake up in Manhattan.

That's how Caleña described it to me, as if getting rich was as natural as simply going to bed at night and waking up in the morning. At that moment, I thought I saw Papa standing behind the counter, not questioning me about what she was suggesting I do or pointing me down the right path like a guardian angel. I thought I saw him in the shadows, working, that's all, scratching his neck in a gesture of tiredness, and thinking about God knows what. Maybe me.

"Maybe you should just keep helping me find her," I told her.

Caleña sighed just to be sighing. We clicked our bottles together to toast to nothing. To toast just to be toasting, an excuse to drink.

"Come here," she said. "Give me your hand."

She took it and without the slightest hesitation, she pulled it over to her legs and without letting go for a second, slid it down onto her cunt that was burning like a furnace.

"You feel?" she told me. "I'm going to get dehydrated, my love."

As usual, she wasn't wearing any underwear. I felt her pulsating like a heart.

"You're soaking wet, Caleña."

"Because of you."

For one second I thought of staying with Caleña and enjoying her wetness. But the following second, I pulled away my hand, which smelled like the sea at night, and wiped it on the tablecloth.

"So, my love?" she asked, trying to catch her breath.

I remembered Milagros waiting for me on the bed, lying down and looking up at the ceiling that was lit up by the streetlight. Maybe as hot as Caleña but quieter about it, stretched out in silence, letting herself be lulled to sleep as I kept telling her my story, in a quieter voice now that I had finally decided to come into her house.

"Yesterday I fell asleep in Mexico," Milagros told me.

"You always fall asleep."

"Tell me more."

"Where did I leave off?"

"It doesn't matter," she told me. "Tell me whatever you want."

Something that won't frighten you, Milagros, so you can go to sleep peacefully. Because I'll have to tell you about the dead, about holes and coffins, about how everything wasn't like in Reynosa, more alive at night than during the day, full of bars and restaurants, noise and music, gringos and whores. The story of the border is a story of shouting and shooting, a story of infamy.

"If I get scared, you'll just have to spend the night," Milagros said.

Just after midnight we went downstairs and they took us out the back door of the hotel, all of us dressed in black, looking like a flock of buzzards. Outside, we got into the back of an old truck that was covered with a tarp. We couldn't see anything; all we heard was Reynosa's ongoing party. Soon it was obvious we had left the paved road; we were now riding slowly on dirt. We were getting pretty shaken up, but we kept quiet until we stopped and they told us to get out. There was a shack out there in the middle of the desert and in the middle of the night, completely dark. The people riding in the cab of the truck ordered us to get off and go inside. There we found others sitting in the darkness.

"You're frightening me," Milagros said. "But you know that."

We waited for a long time. At one point, Reina freaked out because I couldn't tell her how long we'd been there. Give me your watch, she said to me irritably, and she put it on, as if she was letting me know that from then on she would be in charge of time. Nobody talked; some people whispered, as if this was a way to shake off some of their fear.

Milagros pressed up against my body.

Then we heard a vehicle approaching. It stopped in front of the shack. When they turned off the motor, all we could hear was the sound of static on the radio. Then we heard voices and laughter, but all the noises seemed to be coming from different directions. We looked at one another in silence—well, we couldn't actually see anybody else's eyes, but I felt like we were all trying to. Reina was clinging to me the way you are now. Then, all of a sudden, they threw the door open. In the middle of all the noise and confusion, we somehow understood that we had to leave.

Because we didn't understand what they were saying: they were talking in Mexican. Something about the *clica* and the *rucos* and the *morros* and the *cholos*, and the *batos* and a *tecate* and *tu madre*, and what *tons* here and those *chalangos* there, *chingas* and *chingadas*, the *jaina* and the *ranfla*, a *puta* and a *piruja*, and the *placa*, and who the hell gives a flying fuck. It could have been Chinese.

"Did you understand anything they said, Reina?" I asked her.

"Only *puta* and *madre* and *puta madre*," she answered.

There were three of them and they were drunk. One had gold teeth, and the others had gold hanging around their necks. Two were Mexicans and one was a gringo. They never stopped talking and laughing among themselves and coming on to the women who were with us. We were paying so much attention to the liberties they were taking that we didn't notice the truck they arrived in. It was a long flatbed truck carrying huge logs. That's what we were going over in, but we didn't understand, not because they spoke different Spanish or because one of them was a gringo, but because it seemed completely and totally impossible for us to fit in between the logs. So they spoke slowly to make us understand.

"Slowly, like with a burro," one said, and the other two cracked up.

"Fucking burros, burritos, and tacos," said the gringo, bursting with booze and laughter.

Let's see, Milagros, if I can explain how they fit us in. Are you still awake? Very awake and with her eyes wide open. Let's see, here goes: The logs were lying on the truck bed, and from where we were standing behind it, we could see some gaps between them.

"Wait," Milagros asked. "Go slowly, like with a burro."

In the back of the truck, the stack of wood was kind of like Swiss cheese, with big deep holes where we were supposedly going to fit in. Just imagine if you had to go hide in holes dug in a graveyard. One grave per person, where we would be alone and squooshed in, as if we were being buried facedown.

Milagros placed her leg in between mine and nestled her forehead into my shoulder.

Obviously we raised hell, I told her, but just like all the other times, it didn't do us any good. There were eight of us, and half were already crying. A little later we were all practically crying because the coyote said that before getting in we'd have to pay him. For the border guards, he said; he'd have to give them something if they caught us.

"How much?" we asked them.

"Until my hat is full," said the one with gold teeth as he placed a huge sombrero in front of us.

"*Vamos!*" the gringo said, speaking those words in Spanish as if he was spitting them out. "Fill the hat of my *amigo. Todos! Ya!*"

We stood there for a long time because the sombrero remained only half full. They kept saying they wouldn't take off until it was full, that the later it got the worse it was because later, one of them said, they put more guards on duty. Reina stuck her hand down her pants and pulled out three more bills.

"Don't believe them, Reina," I told her. "They're just telling more lies so they can squeeze more money out of us."

"I'm going over no matter what," she said, then shouted at the others. "You want to stay here or what? Let's go, already," she begged them tearfully. "We're just a few steps away. As soon as we get there, they won't steal from us anymore."

"Eh, eh, eh," one of them said. "Watch your mouth, *mujer*, nobody here is stealing from anybody."

The hat filled up very slowly. Just like when priests collect money during mass, that's how the coyotes paced around, laughing like hyenas. Then, when they finally felt like it, they said: Okay, let's see who gets in first.

Reina was the first to move. I saw her climb up and into her hole like a lizard slipping into hiding. The coyote shined a lantern on her and the last thing I saw was the soles of her shoes. Then they lifted up some shorter logs, others got in, and they covered up the holes as if they were setting gravestones. All we needed was some flowers and a relative to cry for us.

I wanted to be near her; I told them I was ready and picked a hole under hers. I slid into the dark tunnel then decided to go back out to see if that pile was going to collapse. But before I could get out, they had already covered me with another log, and there I was, like one more slab of wood.

Then the others got in. I talked to Reina, asked her how she was doing, and through the tree trunks I heard her voice and her answer: She was fine and how was I and she loved me. Suddenly I felt air coming in from somewhere, and it wasn't quite so dark and narrow. Reina loved me, what else did I care about? Anyway, in half an hour everything will have ended, according to what they told us.

"Everybody keep quiet," they ordered.

"*Vámonos,*" said the gringo.

Nobody was allowed to speak along the way. They would let us know when we arrived. It was impossible to keep track of half an hour loaded in the way we were, but there, like cigarettes in a pack, was where I felt the entire weight of our lightness.

My heart almost stopped when I heard the engine start.

It was impossible to stay awake any longer. I knew that sooner or later my tiredness would win out. I didn't even notice when that boy got off; now I'm alone and the seat is empty, as if it was reserved for her. It's a gray afternoon, and the driver announces that we will soon arrive in West Palm Beach.

I definitely don't want to see her without first telling her that I'm coming. After all, I think Patricia was right, it would have been better to let her know to expect me, to arrive with the confidence a real invitation would give me. But nobody answers, just the machine with her voice: Hi, please leave your name and a message . . .

"I'm going to do something for you, son."

"What, Don Pastor?"

"A waiter is leaving, and I thought that you might want to take his place."

Now that really was doing something for me. Getting me out of the sewer, into the light, letting me replace the smell of shit with the smell of food, even though food and shit end up as the same thing in the same place.

"Really, Don Pastor?"

"Let's see if these fit," Patricia said, and handed me a bag with the cowboy uniform: a poncho, belt pouch, *alpargatas*, white canvas pants, and a hat I immediately placed on my head to celebrate my good luck.

"How do I look?"

"Terrible," said Pastor Gómez. "You'd look much better if you were working."

"It's a deal?" I asked them.

They both nodded and smiled and I thanked them. Now I wouldn't have to lie to my family. I would call them that very night and tell them that I was rising in the ranks, that New York was treating me well.

"I didn't know that being a waiter was a career," Papa said that night.

"What I mean is that I'm moving ahead."

"I don't know, son, it sounds to me like you're moving backward."

Milagros also wouldn't have to lie to her aunt and uncle, her four cousins, and the other three relatives who lived with her and who gave me dirty looks whenever we went out. It made her really happy and she gave me two kisses. I'll be earning a little more, too, I told her after I added up my wages plus my tips.

"I'm the one who brought you good luck," she said, wanting to say something else.

And Reina . . . maybe she would laugh at me if she saw me in that costume that represented everything she hated so much. But at least she wouldn't find me defeated, on my knees in front of a toilet bowl.

Milagros suggested we celebrate, and seeing as how there was a good excuse, I agreed. The night was freezing, but when we got to the place she liked to go dancing, the cold was beaten back by the tropical beat. Dozens of Latinos were twisting and turning to the sounds of trumpets and drums. All you could see were legs moving to a frenzied beat, women in bright red clothes and ten-inch heels, lots of perfume, gallons of sweat, men dressed in white or yellow or any other color that made a sharp contrast with the sunglasses they wore even though it was dark. And in the middle of it all, just one of the crowd, was Milagros Valdés, swinging her hips, shaking her shoulders, twisting her legs and arms. And I . . .

"Let me guess," Giovanny Fonseca interrupted me. "You were thinking about the one who abandoned you."

I didn't admit to him that from time to time that night I thought about Reina and at moments missed her intensely. It all depended on the tune the orchestra played and the rum Milagros served me to get my legs moving in time to the rhythm, but then they'd get all wobbly when I'd start to imagine I saw Reina in the crowd.

I couldn't get free of her even when Milagros and I walked out snuggling against each other, against the cold, wrapped in each other and the rum we had drunk. I was going to leave her at her front door, but when we got there, she grabbed my hand and dragged me inside. She told me she wasn't going to let me go, and because of the mood we were both in, I let her lead me into her room, where we fell on her bed; I let her take off my heavy winter clothes; I let her give me the long-dreamed-of kisses; we shared our tongues and our saliva and our bad breath from drinking too much and eating too little.

But when she took off her satin underwear and pressed her hard thighs against me, Reina was there in between us, also naked, just like she was that night she stole the dollars from Halver and Aunt Marlén. Drunk and happy, with the roll of bills in her cunt, she led me into her room, taking advantage of the fact that it was late and Gonzalo was asleep with the television on, but more than anything, taking advantage of her happiness. She said: Sit down there in front of the bed, and like a little girl, she started jumping up and down on the mattress. She kept jumping while she stripped off her clothes until the only thing she was wearing was her panties stuffed with dollar bills. I didn't know whether to look at her eyes or her tits, but the round gaze of her nipples hypnotized me. Reina said to me: Come here, come closer, and I stood up, and from above and with the voice of a girl prostitute, she insisted: Come on, Marlon, come touch me. I approached her, wrapped my arms around her legs, kissed her belly button, slipped my hand under her panties, but all I felt was bills instead of skin. Then she lowered her panties and the dollars fell onto the bed, and it was like she was playing with water, she tossed them up, over herself, and shouted with joy, completely naked, showering herself with money. I tore off my clothes and Reina opened her eyes and her mouth when she saw the size of my erection; she'd never seen me like that. I wanted to take her and squeeze her tight against me and do what I was dying to do, but as soon as she felt me losing control, she said: Stop, Marlon, don't. But Reina, I complained, and she said: No buts, let's leave this for when we get there.

In New York, she appeared in front of me like a ghost to humiliate me while I was doing with another woman what she wouldn't let me do that time with her. But Milagros had decided to fight the ghost, woman to woman. There, on top of me, she let herself go, abandoned herself to her passion. Milagros's excitement made me lose control, and I let myself be carried away by the wondrous things she did with me there in her bed. Here, there, everywhere, upside down and backward, from above and below, things I never even imagined possible.

When we finished, exhausted, she lay her head on my chest as if it was a pillow, and still panting, she said: I love you, Marlon. And I, still in spasms, answered:

"I do, too." But immediately I countered that with "I have to go."

She didn't say anything when I jumped out of bed. I looked for my clothes on the floor, thinking: A person is not always who he is, we don't always agree with what we ourselves say. I looked out the window and suddenly felt all the turmoil that was going on inside me. I approached the glass, naked as I was, and saw that a little piece of Reina's dream was falling from the sky: it was the sight those of us born among mangoes and coconuts long for. I felt both miserable and in awe when I saw that it was beginning to snow.

On New Year's Day, I cursed Reina. I went out very early to take a walk because I wanted to feel under my own feet the snow that had made her so excited. But more than anything, I wanted to shake off the feelings I'd woken up with. I felt angry at life, but a blast of the freezing January wind was like a warning to me to call things by their true names. Finally I realized I was feeling angry at Reina.

I had thought she would appear on Christmas Day, that she would feel trapped by the cold and her own longing and she would call her house to say hi to Gonzalo. But it didn't matter what season it was: Reina remained silent and didn't even appear for New Year's.

"I don't know if I'll ever be able to forgive her for so much ingratitude," Gonzalo told me.

"Maybe she has some problem that makes it impossible for her to call," I said in her defense.

"And what problem might that be? You've also had problems, but it never prevented you from calling."

That Christmas was very different from the ones I was used

to having at home, with fireworks and music that brought good cheer no matter what else was going on. Patricia tried to make up for the lack of the warmth of hearth and home by preparing all the traditional Christmas dishes, as if you could replace your heart with a *buñuelo*.

And since Milagros was born to bring happiness to those around her, she cheered me up during this difficult period. Not only did she distract me with her music and her songs, but I visited her frequently in her room, where I let myself be caressed, let myself be undressed, let myself be loved. I let myself, but . . .

I spent the whole time getting change and standing in line to make the call. Somebody picked up the phone, but nobody spoke. My foot was shaking because this time it wasn't an answering machine. Somebody must be home. Reina, I said, Reina, Reina, but whoever it was hung up. The taped voice of the operator came on asking for more money, and I shoved the coins in the slot, hoping again that somebody would answer. Reina? But whoever was picking up was hanging up, too, without even realizing who was on the other end. Maybe it was Reina and she was half asleep, maybe she'd gotten home from work and just wanted to rest, just wanted the phone to stop ringing. I wasn't going to miss the bus just so I could stand there and keep dialing, but I tried one more time to make sure I wasn't dialing the wrong number; and again: Reina? Reina? And again the person hung up.

I rushed back to the bus. I was just about to leave, complains an older woman sitting in the driver's seat, looking like she really was ready to go. She says to me: You cut your face. Then she grabs the microphone and speaks into it.

"Okay," says the driver, "the next stop is the last stop. We'll be in Miami in a few hours."

And I think: If my foot doesn't stop shaking, I won't be able to get off the bus.

Your foot moves while you're sleeping, Milagros told me. Did it wake you up? I asked her. No, I've been awake and watching you sleep. You really shouldn't, I told her; watching someone sleep is like watching someone take a shit.

"I've got to go," I told her.

"It's still early," Milagros complained. "Keep telling me the story."

"It's been about a month since I've told you anything. I don't even know where I left off."

"Were you already here or were you still there?"

You don't realize when you cross over, Milagros; it's like on your birthday when you look in the mirror and you don't see anything different, but one more year has passed and time has taken its toll. We might have crossed the border at any given moment and none of us would have realized it. There was no way to see out from where we were stuck in between the logs. Anyway, I don't know why, but I kept my eyes closed the whole way, thinking about everything that might happen to us, the stories we had heard about cops and gringos who practiced hunting with illegal immigrants.

"Like they were foxes?" Milagros asked.

I think foxes have more rights near the border. You can't imagine the condition we were in when we arrived. The truck stopped two more times, and both times we thought we'd had it, that our time was up. We heard people talking, but we didn't understand anything. When they started up again, we thought we'd crossed, but a while later they stopped again, and again we heard voices. At some point the truck started driving at full speed down a road full of potholes. The logs started shifting around and we were just like the logs and our bodies were getting banged around against the rough wood. Our clothes didn't protect us at all from big splinters. Some people started shouting, not caring if they found us, and when I realized that one more shout wouldn't increase our danger, I shouted to Reina to ask her how she was, if she felt like raw meat, like I did, if everything was hurting her, like it was me, and if she thought, also like me, that everything had come to an end and we were going to die in that truck.

Reina was okay, or at least she was better off than me. Calm down, Marlon, nothing is going to happen to us. But it seemed like the truck was going out of control, and the pain and the shouting only scared me more. I'm not one to pray, but I prayed, and I even asked to be forgiven for having once wished for a virus that would exterminate all the priests on earth, including the Pope; I prayed really hard for this nightmare to end, for better or for worse, but for it all to end.

"We're there," somebody said.

I heard the logs making the same sound they made while they were sticking us in, and then I heard a voice behind my feet. On the ground, it said to me, but I felt an intense burning sensation when I tried to move. I can't move, I said to whoever was talking to me; then he suggested: Well, you can stay there if you want; and I begged him: No, help me out. He grabbed my feet and pulled me out as if I was being born backward.

Outside, others were on the ground moaning, and Caleña was vomiting into a bush. Then Reina got out, with one shoe on and the other in her hand, her arms all scratched up, her shirt torn, her forehead and nose covered with cuts. She grabbed me and said in a state of ecstasy: We made it, Marlon, we're in the United States; and I, who could barely stand up or hold her up, said: But look how we've ended up; and she added: It doesn't matter, Marlon, we're here. I found enough strength to give her a hug and share her happiness, which I didn't feel, but because it was Reina's happiness, it was worth participating in.

Suddenly we realized there was a ruckus going on: Caleña was whacking the coyotes with a branch and cursing them. You sons of bitches, lying *bandidos*, that's how you treat a woman?! She shouted at them about her injuries, about how badly she'd been treated, how she'd been thrown around, but they thought it was all very funny; it didn't seem like it made them feel guilty at all, and they were laughing and slapping each other on the back and actually enjoying Caleña's tantrum, until one of them got very serious and ordered us to get in a line and start walking. There were more complaints, but by now our voices were pretty weak, and compared to their cursing and insults, you could barely hear us. They kept repeating a bunch of words that sounded to us like their mantras: *que pinchi, que felones y gandallas, que por grifo, que qué onda mi carnal, que por culeros, que qué pedo, que de pilones*.

"I understood *pedo*, that means fart, like it does for us," Reina told me.

"I thought they were speaking English, not Mexican," I told her, and we started walking.

We walked like cows on their way out to pasture; we were herded together so we wouldn't run into the Border Patrol and were prodded on by the idea that we were making this one last effort. How much farther? Is there much farther? We asked them every other minute, but they answered by swearing at us and ordering us to shut up.

From far away we could see the lights of a few houses. Reina turned to me: Those are lights of the United States, and she walked faster so she could be the first to get there. A man near her announced that we would go to one of them, but we had to keep totally quiet. The neighbors don't know anything, he said, and we'd better not wake them up.

We went in without talking, very careful not to make any noise. We followed a gringa who looked like a sweet grandmother type into the back of the house, where they put us into a small room. Wait for instructions and don't talk, the coyotes whispered to us. Then they said good-bye and laughed: Welcome to the United States of America.

In silence we watched the sunrise and nodded off from time to time, but we always stayed alert to any movement or sound. The woman showed up early to look in on us, more out of habit than curiosity; she didn't say or do anything, but a while later she came back with iodine and cotton for us to clean our wounds. We couldn't stop ourselves: we screamed our heads off when we put the iodine on. The woman showed up again, this time with a more irritated look on her face. Someone said to her: *Tenemos hambre, señora*, and she answered without even blinking: I don't speak Spanish. *Hambre*, we said slowly and breaking it up into syllables, *ham-bre*, but we didn't know if she understood that we were hungry, because she walked out, laughing her head off.

We spent the whole day sitting on the floor, mumbling one complaint after another, trying in whispers to figure out what was going on, listening to our guts twisting and turning. At about five o'clock the woman returned with a big bag full of hamburgers. The smell of food picked up our spirits and our instincts: we threw ourselves on the bag like a pack of animals. Luckily there was enough for everyone; there was even one extra piece of meat because the Chinaman ate only the bread.

"Where did he come from?" Reina asked me.

"I think he was in the truck," I told her.

"Maybe, but I didn't realize he was Chinese."

"It looks like he doesn't eat meat."

"Vegetarians are pains in the ass," Reina said.

They fed us because the trip wasn't over yet. Early in the evening, a gringo who spoke very good Spanish showed up, or maybe he was a Mexican who was already forgetting his language. In any case he asked: Who's going to Los Angeles? And off he went with two of the group. A while later, he came back asking for those going to Miami, and finally, well into the night, he came in and asked: And who's going to New York?

We got into the car—Reina, me, and the Chinaman—but then Caleña showed up and said she was going, too.

"Where do you think you're going?" Reina asked her in a nasty voice.

"And what's it to you?"

"Where are you going?" the driver asked Caleña.

"We'll just have to wait and see," she answered flirtatiously.

She got in front with him, and Reina and I and the Chinaman sat in the back. What's your name? Caleña asked the driver. Bill, he said. Then the Chinaman, who hadn't said a word yet, got all excited and said that his name used to be Ping but that from now on he would be called Bill; Chinaman Bill, Caleña said, and started to laugh. The gringo laughed, too, and pushed on the gas pedal so we'd get to San Antonio faster, and from there we took a bus two days later that brought us here.

Milagros got as quiet as me. We were naked under the covers. Her skin was so warm and I thought how delicious it would be to stay, to not go out into the freezing cold.

"I've got to go," I told her.

Milagros pressed up more tightly against me and with the voice of a child who had just woken up, she asked me to stay. I put my nose into her hair and smelled the sweet smell of shampoo. Stay until the morning, she insisted tenderly, half asleep. I thought about how cold it would be outside, and I said:

"All right, I'll stay tonight."

They say that the best part of winter is waiting for spring. For me, the best part was my nights with Milagros Valdés, those hours I spent buried in her warmth, far away from the cold that cut like knives into anybody outside.

Every night after work I faced the freezing wind, thinking about my reward: to spend a few hours with her, even if I did leave later on in the early hours of the morning to go to Giovanny's to stay in a corner with his children.

"It's not that I'm throwing you out, brother," he would say, "but why don't you just stay there with her once and for all?"

I'd tell him about how Milagros got undressed in front of me, how she slept almost naked, wearing only those little tanga panties that split her ass in two. Just a little strap that separated her buttocks and a triangle of cloth that covered the triangle of hair that wasn't supposed to show. That's how I left her every night, half asleep, with her camisole rolled up around her body, a very sexy one that let me see all of her most delicious attributes.

"She even sings in the shower," I told Giovanny.

"Why do you tell me all these things?" he complained. "To

mortify my flesh or to prove to me over and over again what a total ass you are?"

For me it was enough to be with her every night for a few hours. I didn't need anything else to begin to reconcile myself to New York; you need a lot of affection to understand this city. For me, what Milagros gave me was enough, in spite of the danger that Reina might suddenly appear at any moment.

"She's probably got a whole other life by now," Giovanny said.

"You don't like her, do you?"

"The only woman I like without seeing is the Virgin Mary. Anyway, this Reina of yours doesn't even like herself."

"I love her."

"That's what you think," he said.

Even Sundays lost some of their viscosity when I spent them with Milagros. We went for long walks in the city and it was like she was teaching it to me little by little so I wouldn't ever get lost on any street corner, or she was trying to make me fall in love first with the city and then with her.

"You've never seen Manhattan from the clouds?" she asked me.

"From an airplane?"

"Almost," she said, and invited me to go to the top of the Empire State Building.

"And you've never listened to music in the trees?"

"In a forest?"

Not exactly, but she took me to hear a concert in Central Park.

"I'm going to audition with an orchestra," she told me one afternoon.

"To sing?"

"Yes," she said proudly. "They're looking for someone with a voice like mine."

Her dream was to have her own band. Milagros Valdés and the Simpáticos, she told me she would baptize it, but that would only be at first, because afterward she'd sing alone and would be only Milagros Valdés, and when she was famous she would simply be called Milagros, period, just like everybody knows who Celia is, she said.

"I'd also like to study, Milagros."

"Aha!" she exclaimed with that particular lilt in her voice typical of people from the coast of Colombia. "So what are you waiting for?"

For Reina to appear, I thought. But why? I asked myself. I couldn't answer that, but I did know that until I found her, I'd never be free. Maybe that's why I've started to hate myself.

"It already smells like spring," Milagros said.

"That's one thing that comes on its own without you having to look for it," I said.

"What's the matter?"

"Nothing."

Spring brings something besides flowers, besides Milagros's miracles and the longer and longer hours I spend in her bed, which I still went running out of at dawn. In the spring there are also thunderstorms, and Caleña struck Tierra Colombiana like a lightning bolt.

"Have a seat, sugarplum."

"Caleña! What are you doing here?"

"Sit down, because you're not going to be able to stay on your feet."

I took off my sombrero and sat down to face her very worried expression. What happened, Caleña? I managed to ask her. She dug around in her purse, found a little piece of paper, and held it out to me.

"You found her?"

Caleña nodded in silence. I threw my head back and saw stars. I put my hand over my mouth, which had suddenly gotten very cold and dry.

"Are you sure?"

Caleña nodded again. As sure as my name is Luz, she said, and again held the piece of paper out to me. What's the matter with you? Aren't you happy? she asked me.

An eerie silence took hold of the restaurant. It felt to me like everybody had frozen in place, just waiting for me to answer her question. Above everything floated Giovanny Fonseca's enormous eyes. I looked down at the table and saw that it was empty, that we still hadn't put out the napkins and salt and pepper shakers and salsas. Yes, there was an empty space, and I let my head fall onto my arms as if I was passing out in a drunken stupor. Caleña patted my head and I got my snot and drool all over the table. I stayed like that until the silence was broken by the sizzling of empanadas falling into the hot oil, and Pastor Gómez's shout: What's going on here?

"Here," Caleña said to me, "this piece of paper is starting to get on my nerves."

Reina was there in those scribbled numbers and letters.

"Don't you tell her it was me who found her, you hear?" she said, handing me the picture I had given her. "Remember, she doesn't like me."

"But are you sure?"

"Oh, my love, you really are a pain in the ass. If it's not her, you come back here, and I'll hang myself."

Everybody went back about their business, but they kept their ears open for further developments. The only one who didn't move, who was still digesting the news, was Giovanny; we looked at each other with kindred emotions.

"Well, I gotta go."

"You want a beer, Caleña?"

She closed her imitation Chanel bag and stood up. She smoothed out her skirt and said she had to go to some kind of rehearsal or audition.

"Don't blow it, my love. Don't say it was me."

She planted a kiss at the edge of my mouth, then wiped my cheek off with her thumb. She swished over to the door and didn't turn around when I shouted out: Thanks, Caleña.

If Caleña was the lightning bolt, next came the storm, the tempest that dragged me in less than a day to this bus that is now inching its way through heavy traffic as it approaches Miami. I carry with me the vivid memory of the upheaval I left behind me during those final hours, similar to what I caused with my arrival a year ago. But nothing could change the decision I made the second Caleña left my sight: Tomorrow I'm going to find her.

Everyone had an opinion. Call her first. No, better to surprise her. Some said yes; some said no. I should make sure it was her and not somebody who looked like her. In that buzzing hive only two people kept quiet, looking at me, aware of how determined I was. But it was precisely their advice—Patricia's and Giovanny's—I needed most.

"What should I do?" I asked them.

"Call first to see if it's her," Patricia said.

"And to find out if she wants to see you," Giovanny suggested.

I grabbed some coins and went to the phone booth on the corner to call. I managed to control the trembling in my leg and in my fingers while I was dialing, but when the phone started ringing, my whole body started shaking. I leaned against whatever was there, because otherwise I would have fallen for sure. I was standing up on one leg. The other was in convulsions like a wounded snake. I was so confused I even talked to it: Keep still, you blasted leg. But the longer the phone rang, the more it shook, until I managed to push it against the floor with all my strength and step on it with the other foot, pinning it down like it was an animal trying to escape. It rang and I took a breath, because I had forgotten to breathe. Finally I heard Reina's voice.

"Hello?" I said immediately, feeling like I was choking.

It was her voice, but it wasn't her. It was Reina on an answering machine asking the caller to leave his name and a message. I didn't leave anything. I hung up before the beep you are supposed to talk after. It was her voice in clear and perfect English. I'd found her. I don't know why I started laughing, a harsh, joyless laugh, but it was laughter after all. It's a good thing lots of people laugh and talk to themselves in New York City, because there I was, just one more crazy guy. I laughed and jumped up and down around the telephone as if I had just won the lottery. I had won. Finding a lost person in the United States is a lot like picking the right number among hundreds of millions.

I dialed again, again I heard her hoarse, childlike voice, with that Colombian accent that would still be there whether she was talking in Russian or English. I dialed again, fifteen more times, until I ran out of coins. Then I went back to the restaurant; I met up with Don Pastor at the door.

"What happened, son?"

"It's her."

"Did you talk?"

"No, but it was her voice on the tape."

"Are you sure?"

"Absolutely sure, Don Pastor."

He put his arm around my shoulder and suggested we go inside. There was a false sense of normalcy there, everybody pretending to be going about their business, but all the time constantly looking over at us. Don Pastor led me into his office and asked Patricia to join us.

"What are you planning to do?" he asked.

"I'm going to go to her."

"Why don't you talk to her first?" Patricia suggested.

"These aren't the kinds of things you can talk about on the telephone," I told her.

"Marlon is right," Don Pastor said. "As we say back home, only saints can work long-distance miracles."

"I don't know," Patricia said, "but I think it's better if you warn her that you're on your way."

"I'm going to call her, but I'm also going to go."

"What are you going to say to her when you see her?" Don Pastor asked me.

"I don't know," I told him. "Maybe I won't say anything."

"They're going to hug," Patricia said with a lot of emotion.

“I guess,” I said. The three of us stood there in silence.

“When are you going?” Don Pastor asked after a moment.

“Tomorrow,” I told them.

“And what about Milagros?”

Like every night, Milagros waited for me to come from work so she could shower me with love and attention. That night I arrived late because I walked slowly, trying to find words that would hurt less, but when I reached her door, I still hadn’t found them, because they simply didn’t exist. She greeted me as usual. I still got excited and my heart beat faster whenever I saw her. But not that night.

There were no excuses to give Milagros, not one sentence that had any meaning, not one possible explanation. I wanted to say something like “If I don’t find her, Milagros, I’ll just keep being lost forever,” but in the middle of it all, that seemed pointless, too. Silence spoke for me, and that silence made her throw herself on the bed, bury her head under the pillow, and groan, biting the sheet: No, never again, I’m never going to sing again. There was no hug, no possible way to say good-bye to such a woman, a one-of-a-kind woman, no good-bye good enough for her, not even a way to say thank you for giving me the best memories I took with me from New York.

Outside on the street, I thought that maybe I would have done better to keep being lost; here I thought I found one, but then I lost the other, and then I started thinking about keeping my balance, about injustice and all that other bullshit that’s only good for thinking about, and I watched myself dialing the number again of the woman who had finally appeared and again the machine answered. I didn’t leave a message and I called again, dialing from every telephone I could find between Milagros’s and Giovanny’s house, as if I could erase with each call the path I had taken so many nights.

The lights of Miami bounce off a black cloud. It might decide to start raining at any minute. The taxi driver looks at the piece of paper, mumbles a few words, then looks at me as if trying to figure out how much I can afford. It's about half an hour from here, he tells me; I shrug my shoulders. You want to go for it? he asks me. I'll pay whatever the meter says, I tell him.

The alternative is to take another bus and transfer a couple of times at that hour of the night and in a city I don't know. No, I tell myself, any day but today. I'll have to use the money Patricia gave me yesterday. Here, *mijo*, take this, and without her husband seeing, she put a roll of bills in my hand, not that many, but probably enough to pay for this taxi. Giovanny wanted to do the same, but I didn't let him. No, Giovanny, don't even think of it, you've done everything for me already.

"You're going to need it," he insisted.

"Maybe," I said, "but I'm not going to take it from you."

"So let me give you something else, brother."

"Give me a hug, Giovanny."

We gave each other a bear hug, one of those hugs that are so tight it's like you want to keep with you a piece of the other person. Then I saw his eyes like two enormous lakes and I said: I know we're going to see each other soon, Giovanny. I know, too, bro, he agreed. Then it was Don Pastor's turn, who without much to-do gave me a few pats on the back, a big smile, and said: I'm going to keep your job for you, for a while, just in case. And I thought: Just in case Reina decides to come back with me, but I was pretty sure that she wasn't one to ever return anywhere.

"Call us as soon as you get there," Patricia said.

She led me by my hand to the door, leaned over, and gave me a motherly kiss. You are a saint, *señora*, I told her. Don't call me *señora*, she answered, and get out of here, already; you're going to miss your bus.

It's weird, but now I don't feel anything, as if I left all my fear and awkwardness behind me on the bus. Maybe like a soldier in the middle of a battle who is sure that his fate has already been decided. Or maybe because in this encounter with Reina, fate doesn't have anything to do with it. It was fate that I found her, but what happens from now on is up to her.

"Fifty-one or fifty-two?" the taxi driver asked me.

"Fifty-one."

"That's it, then."

A house just like any other, small like all the others in the neighborhood; a house you'd pass by without noticing, with its little front garden and a light over the door. I recall the address I memorized and check it against the number written on the piece of paper in my hand. I still feel nothing. I've probably stopped being me, and it's somebody else who is pressing the doorbell. Coming! calls a woman from inside. I hear a noise as if somebody has tripped. Coming, she says again, and opens the door.

It's not Reina. She could look like this woman in a few years, but she still isn't her.

"Raquel?" I ask.

"Who the hell are you?"

If Marilyn Monroe hadn't died she might look like Raquel, with her hair the same dyed blond, a kind of dried-out bleached look, the same wrinkles, life's scars all over her face. And probably, just like Raquel, she would have a tattoo of a crown of thorns wrapped around her arm, and she would be drunk, alcohol oozing out of her pores.

"I'm Marlon," I tell her.

Raquel lets out a shrill laugh, staggers, and squints as if she's trying to focus her eyes. She looks me up and down from head to toe; I look her over, too. She is wearing a light bathrobe and high-heeled sandals. When she's finished studying me, she waves her arm over her head and clicks her tongue in disapproval.

"You're a baby," she says.

"Can I see Reina?"

She can't hold herself up on her high heels; she spreads her legs out to keep her balance, then leans against the doorframe.

"Can I see her?" I insist.

"Come in."

It's your average living room, small like the house itself. Maybe it has too many decorations, too many porcelain knickknacks that show a certain kind of extravagance, as if they had set up a dollhouse in a bordello. Put that down, she says, pointing at my bag.

"Want a drink?" she asks.

No, I tell her. Well, I do, she says, and picks up an empty glass but can't find a bottle. Do you see it anywhere? she asks me. She weaves her way into the kitchen. I hear the crashing of pots and pans and then an outburst of laughter.

"It's not there," she says.

There is no sign of Reina, or of anybody else. From another room I hear the sound of a television set, but nobody comes out. Raquel crosses the room and goes through another doorway. I hear her peeing. I walk slowly around the living room, looking at everything, looking for Reina, even if only in a picture.

"Here it is." Raquel appears, holds up the bottle, and says, "I found it in the bathroom."

"Raquel," I tell her, "I need to see Reina."

"Reina's not here."

Raquel throws herself down on the sofa, kicks off her shoes, and lies down with the bottle in one hand and the glass in the other. Just when she looks like she's settling in, she gets up, puts down the bottle, picks up a cigarette, and lights it.

"I bet you don't smoke, either, pretty boy," she says, adding the last two words in English.

If only she knew that the reason I was here was a cigarette. Raquel blows out a puff of smoke and starts to laugh again. I don't know about what, but she seems like she's on the verge of bursting. I sit down and ask her:

"Where is she? Where can I find her?"

Her laughter dies down slowly, she makes herself more comfortable, takes a gulp, and says:

"You really want to see her?"

"Hasn't she told you about me?"

"Of course she told me about you." She tries to get up from the sofa but can't get her balance, and sits back down. "She told me you were a very good boy."

"Did she tell you that we lost each other?"

"Not exactly," she says.

Raquel leaves the cigarette on the corner of the table and again tries to stand up. She spills the drink on herself. Shit, she says, and brushes off her robe.

"What did Reina tell you?" I ask her.

"What do you want to hear? You like Roy Orbison?"

"Raquel . . ."

"I love him . . . ," she sings in English.

She gets down on her knees in front of the stereo and tries to find the right button. First the radio blasts, then there's static, then Roy Orbison. She grabs on to the closest thing, tries to pull herself up, then staggers back to the sofa singing: *Only the lonely, dum, dum, dum, dumby, doo, wah . . .*

"What time will Reina be home?" I ask.

"You're getting to be a real drag, pretty boy."

Raquel takes another swig and sings loudly, *Only the lonely know why I cry*.

"You sure you want to see her?" she asks again.

"I've been looking for her for more than a year, Raquel."

"Pobrecito," she says, and again lets out a loud laugh.

I feel the urge to go through the bedrooms and look for her, find out who is back there watching television, put an end to this game of Raquel's.

"Okay, fine," she says, "let's go find her."

After two tries, she manages to stand up and make her way to the hall. *Oh, oh, oh, oh, wah, only the lonely.* I'm going to change, she says, and stumbles to her bedroom, still singing. I wander around the living room while I'm waiting. Again I look carefully at the pictures hanging on the walls.

"Brandon! Brandon!" Raquel shouts from her room.

Finally I see Reina, almost the same as how she was when I left her, but there's nothing of New York in the picture. There are three pictures of Reina, all in the same place. If this drunk woman could only talk, I'd have already gotten my questions answered.

"Brandon!" she shouts again.

Among the pictures is one of a baby; there are two pictures, two babies. Now I'm beginning to feel something, and I also have the feeling that my foot wants to start shaking.

"Didn't you hear me?" Raquel appears, wearing a short dress; the zipper in the back is open.

"Raquel," I say to her, "these children . . ."

She leans against the wall so she won't fall over from laughter and tries to say something but can't get out any words between laughs. Children, she manages to mutter. When she finally settles down, she goes up to the picture and places her hand on top of it. That's my baby, she says, my baby, she says again, talking stupidly the way adults talk to babies.

"It's yours?" I ask, confused.

There goes my baby, the record plays, *there goes my heart* . . .

She moves awkwardly. I can't tell if she is trying to dance or make corrections for her drunken state. She turns her back toward me.

"*Por favor*, please," she says, and stands still so I can close her zipper. The dress is old and too tight, and the zipper gets stuck right where her black bra looks so stark against her skin.

"Thank you, pretty boy," she says in English.

She goes back to her bedroom, and I look again at the picture of the baby. I look for some likeness. Raquel appears, taller now, perched on extremely high heels.

"Wait for me outside," she says, and seeing that I don't respond, she repeats, "Wait for me outside."

"Can I leave that here?" I ask, pointing to my bag.

Raquel doesn't answer; she simply waves her hand in the air again. I go out, waiting for something to happen.

The black cloud has remained where it was, but the wind has gotten colder, as if spring had not really made up its mind yet. Suddenly I hear the grinding of springs and metal. The garage door begins to open. Slowly I see more and more of Raquel's thin legs stylishly perched on top of her spike heels.

"Help me, Brandon," she says from inside the garage.

I push the door open the rest of the way and see an old car full of scratches and dents.

"Are you going to drive?" I ask, worried.

"What?" she answers defensively. "You think I don't know how?"

She gets in the car, starts up the engine, and lights a cigarette. Get in, she orders me. I tell her: Raquel, you can't drive in this state.

"Okay," she says, "so you stay here."

She puts it in reverse and the car jerks out of the garage. I take advantage of the engine dying to quickly get in. She starts it up again and merges into the road without even looking to see if another car is coming, then brakes sharply, turns on the radio, throws the gearshift back and forth, then pushes her foot down on the accelerator; the whole time she's laughing her head off.

Raquel doesn't pay any attention to traffic lights or street signs. At every intersection I close my eyes and clutch the seat. I say something to her about the way she's driving, but her response is to burst out laughing again. She smokes, she laughs, and she sings as we fly down the streets of Miami. Where are we going? I ask her.

"We're going to kill ourselves!" Raquel answers with another big laugh.

We turn onto a wider street, and the traffic forces her to slow down. I lower the window and take a deep breath. Raquel is now driving slowly, but she's still very distracted, following people walking down the sidewalks with her eyes like she's looking for somebody. She parks in a free space. What's happening? I ask her. She opens her purse and takes out a bottle wrapped in brown paper. Are we there? I ask. Raquel wipes her mouth off with her arm, looks over at the opposite side of the street, and lights another cigarette. I don't see anything, I don't see Reina. Is it here, Raquel? She keeps chugging on the bottle and suddenly, just as off the wall as when she bursts out laughing, she starts to cry. What's going on, Raquel?

I look around to find something or somebody that could be the reason for her tears. I don't see anything, but she stretches her arm out in front of me and points to the sidewalk across the street.

"There she is," she says.

Where, my God, where? I don't see her, I can't see her through all the cars that are going by; Reina is getting lost in the crowd.

"Where?"

"There she is."

Reina emerges from the crowd like in one of the many dreams I've had, just like so many times when I imagined her suddenly appearing in front of me. I see Reina looking distractedly up and down the street, Reina coming out of a dream and becoming a reality. I begin to feel. I open the door, but Raquel begins to whine again, leans on the horn, and starts sobbing. I start to get out, but she grabs my arm and digs her nails into me. Let go of me, Raquel! I try to get away from her. Her sobs turn into fake laughter, like a clown's. Let go of me, damn you! I pull away and tear myself loose, open the door, and get out just opposite Reina, who still isn't paying any attention.

"Reina!" I shout.

The noise of the street drowns out my voice. I try to cross but the cars are rushing by. From outside I can hear Raquel: she is crying again. Reina! I shout, but Raquel has collapsed on the horn, she's leaning on it, and people start turning to look. Reina also turns to find out what the fuss is about and looks right at me; I raise my arm cautiously. Reina, I say quietly. I see that I can cross the street, I walk slowly toward her, with my arm still raised so she won't lose sight of me. Reina lifts her arm and stops a taxi, talks to the driver through the window without looking back at me. She gets in the taxi. I speed up and begin to shout: Reina, wait for me! The taxi takes off with her in it, and I run behind it. Reina doesn't even turn around. I keep running, but the taxi pulls out ahead. I keep running, flying, like only I know how to run. The taxi gets farther away, and I keep running behind it.

Almost totally out of breath, I shout: Stop, Reina! Stop, you bitch, you whore! You fucking thief!

"Your foot is shaking."

I went back to Reina's house and I tried to see in the window if there was anybody there, maybe whoever was watching television, or whoever was taking care of the baby, or Raquel's boyfriend, the one she left Gonzalo for, left everything for, even her daughter. Somebody to tell that the lady is in a parked car next to the sidewalk, drunk, sleeping in the car with the radio on, the lights on, pissing on the seat, vomiting her guts out onto the steering wheel. I'm spying through the window, looking for Reina as I never stopped doing until I found her, but it is she who finds me, who surprises me from behind to say to me, as if no time at all has passed:

"Your foot is shaking."

"Sometimes it shakes," I tell her.

"I remember," Reina says.

We are standing a few feet apart, but she takes a step forward and stands under the porch light.

"What happened to your face?" she asks.

"What happened to your eyes?" I ask.

"That's how they should always have been."

They are the same color now. And her hair is blond, not as blond as Raquel's, but as blond as if she'd been born that way. There's something about her that doesn't quite fit, and it's not just that a lot of time has passed.

"Help me get her in the house." She's referring to Raquel.

"How did you find her?" I asked.

"Looking for her."

"Why didn't you look for me?"

Reina walks toward the car, and I follow a few steps behind. Reina tells me: Like she is now, she weighs more than a man. I ask her: Why don't you wake her up? Because she doesn't wake up, she answers. And she drives like that? I ask her. You don't have any right to give your opinion about my mother, Reina says.

She picks her up in her arms, but I have to help. She's completely unconscious, but she's still mumbling nonsense.

"What's she saying?"

"Nothing," Reina says.

I grab her around the waist and throw her over my shoulder as if she was a sack of potatoes. Now Reina is walking behind me. Where do I put her, Reina? Leave her on the sofa. Why not in her room? Because I said so, she answers. Raquel mumbles under her breath: There's no meat for tomorrow.

I let her go, drop her like I couldn't give a damn about her. Her dress has been pushed up, and I see that she's not wearing any underwear, showing a dark bush that doesn't match her blond hair. Reina pulls her dress down and goes outside.

Where are you going?

Reina doesn't answer. Again to the car. She gets in, sits down, and turns off the lights. I wait for her to come out, but she just sits there, looking forward as if she was driving down a straight stretch of road. I lean against the other window, stick my head in, and say: Reina.

"What do you want?" she asks me.

I open the door and sit down, looking ahead, too, as if we

were both driving down a long highway. The radio is still on, and Reina remains silent. She is sitting on her hands.

"Reina . . . that baby."

"The little girl is none of your business, Marlon."

She keeps looking forward as she talks, like she's driving the car and would crash if she looked away. Look at me, Reina, but she doesn't look at me. She clenches her jaw and throws her head back. Look at me, Reina. With her head back, she looks at me.

"Why did you want me to come with you if you were just going to leave me?" I ask her.

"I didn't leave you," she says. "You left and never came back."

"I couldn't . . . I got lost."

Reina lets out a disgusted laugh, just like her mother, and says in English, Oh, my God, then grabs on to the steering wheel with both hands.

"You didn't look for me, Reina."

"Where was I supposed to look for you?"

"The same places I looked for you," I say. "Around."

She turns on the car lights, then turns them off. She turns them on and off.

"If you'd looked for me, you would have found me," I tell her. "Just like you found your mother."

Again she looks straight in front of her and stretches her hand out to the radio, turning the dial to different stations. One of them is playing salsa. Reina keeps turning the dial until she finds something she likes.

"Why didn't you ever call home? Your father is very ill."

"I can still call," she says.

She turns up the radio. She sits on her hands again. The radio announcer says that it is twelve-thirty, it's 69 degrees out, the night is overcast, and there are black clouds in the sky, there's 90 percent humidity, and 99 percent chance of rain. Reina looks at me with those eyes that made me follow her, now identical, the same color, and she says to me:

"You haven't changed a bit, Marlon."

I want to answer but my throat gets all knotted up. At this moment I am one big knot wanting to tell her everything I've been through, tell her that one year is a long time, and even longer if you've been living with fear, tell her that every night I've woken up with a start, that I'm tired as if I hadn't stopped running since that first night she warned me not to go out, that it's exhausting to look and look and not find, that life is exhausting, that everything is exhausting.

"It's tiring to look for you, Reina," I say finally.

"Why didn't you kill yourself?" she says to me with that same old rage. "Why didn't you just kill yourself, Marlon?"

A few drops of rain fall on the windshield as if God was spitting at us for defying His will. Reina is looking at me, her eyes filled with tears, waiting for an answer or maybe waiting for my death. My eyes are filled with tears just like hers.

Today I don't want to die, Reina, because sometimes time is generous and now it is playing fair with me. I've finally stopped looking for you, I'm done with all that; now I understand what I'm doing here with you and why I went out running; now I know a lot more. Can you believe it, that I even understand the pain and uncertainty of being Colombian, and I understand that when you wanted to change countries, Reina, you didn't understand that a person's country is wherever there is love and affection. Now I know where my steps are taking me; I don't have calluses only on my feet. This is time's gift, though the only thing that's changed about you is your eyes.

It's amazing, but my foot isn't shaking anymore. And even though my voice is shaking, I'm going to set it free so I can tell you, now without any anger:

"Go ahead and kill yourself, Reina, if you want to."

I get out of the car and go get my things. The rain falls on my face. Reina remains in the car with her forehead pressed against the steering wheel.